The Total Eclipse of Nestor Lopez

Also by
ADRIANNA CUEVAS

Cuba in My Pocket

The
Total Eclipse
of Nestor Lopez

ADRIANNA CUEVAS

SQUARE
FISH

Farrar Straus Giroux
New York

For Soren, my home

SQUARE
FISH

An imprint of Macmillan Publishing Group, LLC
120 Broadway, New York, NY 10271
mackids.com

Square Fish and the Square Fish logo are trademarks of Macmillan and
are used by Farrar Straus Giroux under license from Macmillan.

Our books may be purchased in bulk for promotional, educational, or
business use. Please contact your local bookseller or the Macmillan Corporate
and Premium Sales Department at (800) 221-7945 ext. 5442 or
by email at MacmillanSpecialMarkets@macmillan.com.

Library of Congress Control Number: 2019948764

Originally published in the United States by Farrar Straus Giroux
First Square Fish edition, 2021
Book designed by Monique Sterling and Mercedes Padró

Square Fish logo designed by Filomena Tuosto

ISBN 978-1-250-79185-6 (paperback)

5   7   9   10   8   6

AR: 4.7 / LEXILE: 740L

The Total Eclipse of NESTOR Lopez

CHAPTER 1

I GRIP DAD'S OLD ARMY COMPASS, willing myself not to launch it at the obnoxious raven heckling me from the bedroom window. I've lived in five other places, but the birds in New Haven are by far the most annoying.

"Did you hear the old lady who lives here cooks raccoons and armadillos for dinner?" the raven chirps, hopping back and forth on the windowsill. He bobs his black head at the packing boxes in my room.

"I know for a fact that's not true." I kick a large cardboard box labeled NESTOR'S COMIC BOOKS AND DART

GUNS under my bed. The springs under the mattress groan as the box pushes against the bed frame. "My abuela is the best cook in Texas."

"Fine. Don't believe me. Maybe I'll visit you in the hospital when they have to remove your small intestine after you eat too much barbecued roadkill."

I roll my eyes. Sometimes being able to speak to animals is not as cool as you would think.

I clench my jaw and shove another box under my bed, getting down on my knees to push against the straining bed frame. This raven is keeping me from breaking my unpacking record. Moving among five Army bases, I've perfected my skills. I hold the record for fastest room packing and unpacking in the entire universe. You can get away with unpacking only one box of clothes for about three weeks before your mom realizes you've been wearing your cat-surfing-on-a-piece-of-pizza T-shirt every day. I know sorting through your boxes in front of a curious new neighbor means he'll see all your underwear and the ratty stuffed bear you still insist on sleeping with.

But the secret to success is not to bother unpacking half your boxes when you get to your new location.

That way you're ready to go when your mom announces the inevitable.

I wasn't surprised when Mom said, "Nestor, we're moving to New Haven, Texas." We'd lived at Fort Hood for six months, I was getting used to my new school, and my classmates were about to earn friend status. My teachers finally started calling me by the right name. I knew that was my cue to get ready to move again.

So two days ago, I set my stopwatch and timed myself as I threw my sketchbooks and pencils into one box, my animal encyclopedia into another, and the remaining dart guns, Legos, and Pokémon cards that had survived the last four moves into a third box. Five minutes and thirty-four seconds!

Although, I forgot to pack my underwear.

The raven pecks at the peeling paint on my windowsill, his thick black feathers shining in the sunlight. He looks like he's covered with oil, a twisty design of green and purple on his wings. I abandon my unpacking and grab my sketchbook so I can draw New Haven's annoying wildlife.

"Oh, so you're gonna make me famous? You even a good artist?" The raven stretches out his feathers.

I consider drawing an enormous black bear devouring the raven, feathers and bird bits flying through the air.

I'm shading in just the right look of obnoxious in the raven's eye when I hear a soft knock on the bedroom door.

My abuela shuffles in, her curly hair piled on her head. She tried to dye it red to cover her gray, but it's come out more of a purple. It matches the tiny flowers on her housecoat.

Abuela gives me a hug, and I inhale the scent of lavender. Of the five times I've moved, this is the first time someone I know has greeted me. Usually it's just an empty house with echoing walls and neighbors' curious eyes. I could stay in Abuela's hug forever.

"And how is the unpacking?" She scans my new room and pauses when she sees the packing boxes shoved under my bed. She chuckles, giving me a wink.

The raven beats his wings against the window frame. "Oh, you are so busted."

I shake my head and look at Abuela, checking to see if she can hear my annoying animal companion, too. She's busy pulling a brown paper bag from behind her back, no reaction on her face. I guess my ability to talk to animals didn't skip a generation.

"Fine, I guess." I glance at the boxes in my closet, shoved behind my clothes.

Abuela takes my sketchbook and holds it at arm's length, admiring my raven drawing. "Ay, mira. Another masterpiece, Joselito."

Abuela likes to call me Joselito sometimes, after José Nicolás de la Escalera. He was Cuba's first painter. Abuela tells me she hopes to see my drawings one day in museums around the world, just like José's. I don't bother to tell her I don't think I'm that good. I draw because it keeps me occupied sitting in new classrooms as the teacher drones on about equations I learned two schools ago.

And paper and pencils are easy to pack.

"What's that?" I ask, as Abuela holds out the brown paper bag to me.

"I have something for you, niño." Abuela's eyes sparkle.

I peek inside. A baseball glove rests at the bottom.

"I thought you might want that. I went up to the attic to dig it out of some boxes. Ay, almost broke my hip, esas tontas escaleras."

I run my fingers over the worn glove, smiling as Abuela curses the attic stairs. The brown leather has cracks in the palm, and a few loose laces hang from the edge. It's definitely well used.

"This glove was your papi's. He and your abuelo spent hours out there in the backyard, tossing a baseball back and forth. I had to yell at them so much to stop throwing and come in for dinner. And I'm a good cook. Ya tú sabes." Abuela chuckles and sits next to me on the bed. She shifts her weight as the boxes crammed under my bed push the sharp bedsprings against the mattress. I hear the cardboard begin to crunch on one of them. I hope that's not the one with my aquarium.

"Gracias, Buela. This is really cool."

My dad's glove. I slide my fingers inside and flex the glove open and closed. I definitely won't forget to pack this when we move again.

Abuela rubs my back and whispers in my ear. "I have something else, mi niño."

"What is it?" I wonder how she's going to top the glove.

She reaches into the pocket of her housecoat and holds out an envelope.

I glance at the white paper in her hand, recognizing the small, all-caps handwriting.

Dad.

My heartbeat pounds in my chest, and I grab the envelope from Abuela.

"No way! Already?"

"I leave you to it." She kisses the top of my head and pads out of the room in her house slippers.

I have an entire shoebox of letters from Dad. The inbox of my email has its own overflowing folder of messages he's sent me over the last three months of his deployment. And yet, every time I get a letter from him, my heart beats so fast I can hardly breathe. I always scan the envelope's return address for some clues about him. Has he moved bases? Is he still in the Middle East? The cryptic combination of letters and numbers on this one tells me he's at Bagram Air Base, Afghanistan.

I tear open the envelope and read.

Nestor,

I know we usually email, but I wanted to have something waiting for you when you got to New Haven. Hopefully, this letter arrived in time.

Specialist Fischer and I played catch yesterday, so I wrote "Kabul, Afghanistan" on your baseball. I'm starting to run out of room on that thing! But I managed to squeeze it in between "Ramstein, Germany" and "Daegu City, South Korea." You and I will have to toss it around when I get home so we can write "New Haven, Texas" on it.

All right. Here's your animal question. There's a species of sheep here in Afghanistan named after a famous explorer. Write me back with the name. I'm pretty sure I've stumped you with this one!

Good luck at your new school. I know you'll do great. You always do.

Love,
Dad

I read the letter three more times, tracing my finger over Dad's signature. I fold it carefully and tuck it between the pages of my sketchbook. There's a golf ball in my throat I try to swallow down.

Three months ago, Mom and I stood on a hot

tarmac and stared at Dad's back as he boarded a big-bellied airplane to Afghanistan. It was our fourth time watching him fly away, his shoulders hunched a little more with each deployment. I gripped Mom's hand, my palm sweaty, and pretended it was the strong sun making my eyes water.

Now Dad is across an ocean, playing catch with someone who is not me. Dad says all this moving, all this being separated, is part of the job. When you're Nestor Lopez, son of Sergeant First Class Raúl Lopez, every time the Army says "move," you move.

And it sucks.

I sigh, picking up my charcoal pencil again to continue shading the raven.

"Wait, wait," he crows on the windowsill. "Get my good side."

He spins around and lifts his back feathers.

I roll my eyes and turn to a clean page of my old sketchbook, flipping past pages labeled Georgia, Colorado, Washington, Kentucky, and Texas. I write *Days in New Haven* at the top of the page and make two tick marks underneath. I wonder how many lines I'll be able to make before we have to move again. I draw a small circle about halfway down the page. That's my guess for when Mom will sit me down with a big sigh and a rub on the back.

"Hey, if you're such a know-it-all, tell me about New Haven. They got anything fun to do? Movie theater? Skate park? A teleportation device that takes you to a better town?"

The raven hops and turns around. "Hoo-eee, it's better than a worm salad for breakfast, I tell you what."

He cranes his neck toward the skateboard thrown in the bottom of my closet. "Pretty cool skate park. Just behind the abandoned Dairy Queen."

I raise my eyebrow. From what I've seen, I'd be lucky if that skate park is anything more than one concrete block and a piece of plywood. Driving into New Haven, Mom accidentally sailed through the town's one stop sign. Not stoplight. Stop *sign*. Several boarded-up windows were plastered with missing-pet flyers on the few buildings downtown. I wonder if the residents of New Haven have forgotten they had formed an actual town and aren't just living next to one another by chance. My obituary will probably read, "Died of boredom in New Haven, Texas."

I've worn down the tip of my black charcoal pencil

and can't find my sharpener. It's probably hiding at the bottom of a box labeled MISMATCHED SOCKS or TOYS I HAVEN'T PLAYED WITH IN SIX YEARS. I move through the boxes scattered in my room and start piling them in the closet. I'm stacking a third box on my tower when I notice writing scrawled on the back wall. *Raúl Armando Lopez's secret hiding spot. Trespassers beware.* The handwriting is shaky, and a stick figure dog is drawn underneath.

I smile at the thought of Dad labeling a hiding spot that's supposed to be secret. I hope the Army has taught him better camouflage since.

I take the box and start a new stack, leaving Dad's message uncovered. I continue stacking my unpacked boxes until they reach the top of the closet. I have to use all my body weight to close the closet doors, the wood creaking against my shoulder as the cardboard crumples.

"All unpacked?" Mom's head pops around the doorframe, and she scans the room.

I jump onto my bed and move my feet in front of the boxes crammed under the frame. I keep an eye on the closet door, praying it stays shut. "Yeah, sure. Of course."

"Look under the bed! Look under the bed!" The raven flaps his wings and squawks.

I snap my head toward the raven and swat at him with my sketchbook. He flies away from the window with a screech.

Mom's tired face doesn't show any hint of understanding the bird. The dark circles under her eyes match the purple in her shirt, and her black hair has mostly fallen out of her messy ponytail, sticking to the sweat on her forehead. It seems like with each move, she gets slower at packing and unpacking, while I get faster. She always saves a picture of Dad in his dress uniform until last, wrapping it in her green-and-gold scarf and placing it in her purse, removing it only when we reach our next destination.

"Let's take a selfie for Dad in your new room," Mom says, sitting next to me on the bed.

Mom is obsessed with taking pictures for my dad. She holds out her phone, and I lean in close to her. Wrapping her arm around me, she taps a button and captures our toothy smiles. I don't have the heart to tell Mom that her arms are so short Dad won't be able to see anything behind us. For all he knows, we could've moved to the surface of Mars.

Mom stands and inspects the picture. She looks at the boxes under my bed, her hand wrapped around Dad's wedding band hanging from a gold chain at her neck. She rubs the ring with her thumb. "Nestor, *actually* unpack this time. I'm serious."

"Yes, ma'am." I look down at my bare feet swinging off the edge of the bed. There's a scar on my right big toe from a bad game of kickball in Kentucky and another scar on my left ankle from a doomed hike in Colorado. "It's not like it matters anyway."

Mom gives me a weak smile. "New Haven will be different. We're not on another military base. Maybe you'll like it."

Fort Hood had a Whataburger, a video arcade, and a comic book shop where you could read as long as you wanted if you bought chips or candy bars from the owner. Most kids at school had parents in the military, so everyone understood if you didn't want to talk in the middle of science because your dad had flown across an ocean the night before. Now Mom's moved me to a town where I'm a circus freak. An alien from a distant planet. My only comfort is knowing I might not be here long.

"Your dad loved growing up here. I know it will be good for you."

"Until the next move." I grip my pencil so hard it snaps in my hand.

Mom sighs and rubs her eyes. "I don't know what to tell you, Nestor. We're here with your abuela. You'll be okay."

I open my mouth to argue just as the old closet doors give way, revealing an avalanche of crushed cardboard and packing tape. Mom's raised eyebrows silence me as I sigh and shuffle over to Mount Packing Box, the dart guns, Legos, and old sketchbooks taunting my unpacking skills. Obviously, no unpacking record will be broken today.

CHAPTER 2

"CHAO, PESCAO," ABUELA CALLS after me as I leave her house.

I wave and shout back, "Y a la vuelta, picadillo!"

I hike my backpack onto my shoulder and head off to school. All I have is my sketchbook, a half-used spiral notebook from my old school, my pencil pouch, and Dad's compass. Mom and Abuela got a school supply list when they registered me, but I ignored it. I probably won't be at New Haven Middle School long enough to use all the things on the list anyway.

As I start up the trail into the woods, a black blur sails above me, diving between tree branches.

"What was that all about?" the raven squawks, buzzing my hair.

"What?" I ask, turning to make sure Abuela's gone back into her house and won't see me chatting up a bird.

"All that Spanish. Don't you know how to say adiós?"

"That's how Abuela and I always say goodbye. Didn't matter if she was calling me on the phone or visiting us in Washington or Kentucky or wherever, we'd say goodbye the same way."

"And what exactly were you saying? You were talking about me, weren't you?"

I shake my head and laugh. "Hardly. Abuela says it has to do with the ration cards they gave out in Cuba when Castro would let people buy only fish one day and beef the next."

"That's not cool."

"Well, he was a dictator, so what do you expect?"

I take Dad's compass out of my backpack and clutch it in my hands.

"What's that?" the raven asks, sailing to the ground

and hopping next to me. So much for a quiet walk to school.

"It's a compass. My dad gave it to me when I was in preschool, before his first deployment."

I rub my thumb over the face of the compass. When I was little, I thought the red needle pointed to Dad instead of north. I would spend hours staring at the face, willing the tiny red arrow to swing toward me.

I didn't want to leave Abuela's house this morning. It wasn't the usual "I don't want to go to school" tantrum. I wanted to stay and take in every wall, every corner of the house. There are lines on the doorframe in the dining room marking Dad's height as he grew up. Abuela has a framed picture of her and Abuelo standing in the living room in their wedding clothes. Her house has a history. It's a home.

I've never lived anywhere like that.

The raven jumps onto a rock and then launches himself into the air. "You know, it's a lot faster to walk through town to get to school."

I scuff my feet on the trail. "I'm not in a hurry. Besides, I figured I could sketch some animals or trees out here. I didn't get to wander much on Army bases."

"You didn't?"

"Well, you never knew if you were going to stumble onto some grenade exercises or bazooka practice." I wink at the raven. "So do you have a name?"

"A what?" The raven brushes his wing on the ground, flinging brown dirt onto my shoe.

"A name. Something people call you."

The raven twists his neck and looks up at me. "You mean like Don't-Poop-on-That or Get-Away-from-My-Cat?"

"Exactly." I think for a moment. I've never had a pet. Mom said they'd be too difficult to have to move all the time. This obnoxious raven is probably the closest I'll ever get. "How about Cuervito?"

"Did you just insult me?"

"No. It's Spanish for 'little raven.' How about I call you that?"

"What about Mr. Cuervito? Or Professor Cuervito?" The raven starts flapping his wings. "Wait . . . Evil Doctor Cuervito!"

"Yeah, I'm just gonna stick with Cuervito."

The raven cranes his head at me. "Fine. And I'll call you Don't-Poop-on-Him."

"Or Nestor."

"Whatever." Cuervito flaps his wings and soars off

the ground. "Be careful in the woods. You might not want to sketch everything."

I raise my eyebrow as Cuervito takes off over the trees and out of sight.

The woods behind Abuela's house are filled with twisty live oak trees and sharp cacti. I look down to make sure I don't impale my shin with spines, but I almost give myself a concussion from the winding tree branches. Good thing Abuela added plenty of sugar to my café con leche this morning.

The path curves up and down small hills, around cedar trees, and through mesquite bushes. It's less hilly than where we lived in Colorado, but hillier than Kentucky. There are fewer trees than in Washington, which was full of tall pines, but more than in the rocky fields at Fort Hood. As I meander down a hill, my worn sneakers slide on the dirt, sending small rocks skittering down the path. I notice movement out of the corner of my eye.

A white-tailed deer stares at me as she munches some grass, her mouth chewing in circles as green sprouts hang from her lips. "Having a good breakfast?" I try to keep my voice soft so she knows I'm not a threat.

The deer pauses her meal and says, "Not particularly. I believe a squirrel peed on this patch."

I chuckle. "Dude, that's gross."

The deer's mouth falls open, and bits of half-chewed grass fall from her teeth.

I'm used to this reaction the first time an animal finds out I can understand it.

"Would you mind if I sketched you?" I ask, sliding my backpack off my shoulder and finding a crook between two tree roots to sit down. I'm not in a hurry to get to school. "You can keep eating your breakfast."

"That would be all right," the deer responds, bending her head down to rip another clump of grass from the dirt.

A small brown rabbit hops from behind the tree and nudges my arm with his twitching nose. "If I stay by you, will you keep it from getting me? You'll keep me safe, right?"

"Um, sure, I guess," I say, flipping through my sketchbook as the rabbit's trembling body presses against my leg.

"I like that one," the rabbit says, nodding at my drawing. His cotton-ball tail won't stop shaking.

I look at the sketch on the page of a mountain goat

perched high on a rock. His head cranes toward the sky as his mouth gapes open. "That's from Colorado. Mom and Dad took me up Pikes Peak when my dad came back from Iraq. Did you know some mountain goats are scared of heights? This one screamed the whole time I sketched him."

The rabbit thumps his foot on the ground.

I turn to a clean page, and a paper drops out of my sketchbook. I open it and smile. *First-Day Challenge* is written at the top in capital letters, with more exclamation points than humanly possible. Mom does this for all my first days of school. I scan the page and see *Introduce yourself to your teachers: 20 points* and *Open your locker in less than a minute: 50 points*. Mom says that if I treat my first days like a video game, they'll be easier.

I don't have the heart to tell her that you can't respawn in real life if you die from eating mystery meat sauce in the cafeteria: thirty points.

I brush my hand over the page in my sketchbook and start drawing the general shape of the deer's body, not bothering to create careful lines.

"Do you want me to give you more muscles? How about a huge set of wings?" I ask the deer, pausing my sketching. "I can pretty much draw you any way you want."

The deer looks at me and blinks her large brown eyes. "I do believe I'm perfect just the way I am."

"Wow, I think her ego is as big as her antlers," the rabbit says, scratching behind his long ears.

"She doesn't have antlers."

"Oh, right." The rabbit looks up at me. "If you concentrate on that drawing any harder, you're going to bite through your lip."

I smile, certain there's a tooth mark on my lower lip. "Sorry. Just thinking about having to start school all over again. Trying to decide who I want to be this time."

"Class clown?" the rabbit offers.

I shake my head. "Tried it. Gets exhausting after a while."

"You seem halfway to slacker," the deer says, raising her head. "How about that? You could forget your homework and sleep in all your classes."

"Probably not." I chuckle. "One phone call home to my mom and that would be over. Fast."

I run through my options. When I was going to school near Fort Lewis in Washington, I decided I'd be an athlete. I played on the soccer team and wore a Seattle Seahawks hoodie to school every day. By the time people figured out I was terrible at soccer and had never watched a single football game at Century-Link Field, Mom and I were already on our way to Fort Campbell. In Kentucky, I pretended I could speak only German. That didn't last long, since I know only five words. Luckily, neither did our posting there.

"I suppose I could just be myself," I tell the rabbit and the deer. "That would be original."

"Dead man walking!" I hear a screech above and see Cuervito has returned to pester me.

"I thought you were too scared to fly through the woods?" I taunt him.

"I was just checking on you. Can't let you miss your first day of school, can I?"

I sigh. "I've had plenty of first days of school. This is no big deal."

"Oh, really?" Cuervito lands on my foot, which is stretched out on the ground. The rabbit snuggles behind my arm.

I flip my sketchbook shut. "The Army doesn't exactly wait to move you until the school year is over. So we've moved a couple of times in the middle of the year. That means I've had nine first days of school. Today is number ten."

"I don't believe you." Cuervito pecks at my shoelace.

I take a deep breath and hold out my hands. "I went to kindergarten and first grade at Fort Benning, Georgia," I say, holding up two fingers. "Next was part of second grade at Fort Carson, Colorado."

"That's three first days," the raven says.

"I'm not done. The rest of second grade and third grade was at Fort Lewis, Washington. Then fourth grade and part of fifth grade was at Fort Campbell, Kentucky."

"Hoo-eee, we're at seven first days."

"I didn't know ravens could count," the deer taunts.

"The last month of fifth grade and the first two months of sixth grade were at Fort Hood, here in Texas."

"Nine! We've got nine!"

I hold up ten fingers. "And now my first day in New Haven."

"You're making me tired, kid," the deer says.

I nod, sliding my sketchbook into my backpack and tucking Dad's compass into my pocket. I brush the dirt off the back of my jeans, and something bright pink next to a tree root catches my eye. There are two plastic tags with the numbers three and eight on them. I'm not sure what they are, but I shove them into my pocket, a souvenir from my first day in the woods.

The rabbit hops next to me as I walk down the path. "First day. That's rough. Just make sure your shoes are tied and your zipper is zipped."

I wave my hand, brushing off the rabbit's comment, but quickly drop my eyes to check my jeans.

I'm good.

"No, no," Cuervito cries overhead, sailing above us. "He's gotta find the biggest, ugliest kid in school."

"And?" the deer asks, following me.

"And punch him in the nose!" Cuervito spins and lands on the deer's back. She kicks her hind legs, launching the raven back into the air.

"Don't listen to him," the deer says. "Just sit in the front row in every single class and raise your hand every time the teacher asks a question. Even if you have to lift yourself out of your seat to wave your hand around like crazy. Trust me."

The animals in New Haven are trying to get me killed.

Cuervito dive-bombs the deer again in a blur of

black feathers. "No, he needs to wait until the class is totally silent. Nobody talking. Everybody hardly breathing." He flies upward and stretches his wings out, sailing in a circle above us.

I sigh. "And?"

"And let 'er rip!"

Groaning, I pick up the pace toward school, my animal entourage following me and offering advice guaranteed to get me a month of detention.

CHAPTER 3

SIXTH GRADE AT MY SIXTH SCHOOL. A maze of rusty lockers, creaking doors, and ceiling tiles stained with muddy brown splotches.

Luckily, most schools in the United States look exactly the same. You think they're prisons until you notice the swings and jungle gym behind the plain, brown brick building with small windows.

The faded sign outside New Haven Middle School declares HOME OF THE FIGHTING ARMADILLOS. The only fighting I've ever seen an armadillo do is against a truck on the highway.

And they usually don't win.

Despite my confidence, I soon realize the classrooms in New Haven Middle School must've been numbered with a confetti cannon. My first-period class, English, is supposed to be in room 17, but walking down the hall, I pass room 11, room 3, and room 19.

In that order.

I try to remember the map the school secretary gave me, now folded in my back pocket. I don't want to take it out. I might as well get on the school's PA system and announce, "New kid lost and wandering the halls!"

The faces rushing past me are all busy talking and laughing as they head to class. No one seems to notice me. At all my other schools, at least one kid always took me under their wing the first day. When I started second grade at Fort Lewis in Washington, Jacob Kilmer spent all morning showing me the activity centers in the classroom and telling me wild stories about the art, music, and PE teachers. Eventually, he got tired of my questions and pretended I was invisible. It was just as well, because I learned a day later that Jacob had come to Fort Lewis just a week before me—so everything he'd told me was wrong.

I finally find my English class by accident, but my nervous bladder tells me to look for the boys' bathroom instead. There's a slight chance I was too confident last night, snoring away under my freshly unpacked blanket, cardboard boxes still forcing the bedsprings to poke my ribs through the mattress.

In English, math, and history, the teachers make me stand in front of the room and introduce myself. I briefly consider pulling the fire alarm instead. At least Mom will be proud I earned some points.

My introductions are greeted with half-hearted waves and mumbles from kids slumped over in their desks. I probably could've announced I was Mr. Whet Faartz and ridden a llama to school without anyone noticing.

After lunch, I sit in my science class, amusing myself while the teacher rambles on about how to calculate density. I sketch Cuervito in my notebook, trying to get the right shade of black for his eyes. A shade of black that says, "I have made it my brief life's mission to annoy the new kid as much as possible."

Apparently, I'm concentrating more on my drawing than on dividing mass by volume. Now my science teacher, Miss Humala, is standing over my desk, craning her long neck. She stretches her jaw and sticks out her lips. Her long red nails twitch as if she wants to snatch my drawing and crumple it into a tiny ball.

"Mr., uh . . ." She pauses, searching her brain for my name. "Mr. Lopez. You really do need to pay attention. Focus, please."

She snaps her fingers and walks back to the front of the room.

I go back to my drawing but look up periodically to check that Miss Humala isn't about to assault me with her spit to get my attention. I'm sitting in the last row, so it's easy to keep an eye on everything. When I walked into class after lunch, I scanned the room and chose a seat in the back, like always. I figured I was doing the teacher a favor. This way, she won't have a gaping seat in the middle of the room when I leave again.

"Oh, look, we have an artist in class," I hear a voice say behind me. "Just don't pet me or pick me up or feed me leftover Tater Tots from the cafeteria, please."

I turn and see a large cage in the corner of the room. Peeking out from a blue fabric hammock strung between two corners of the cage is a small gray chinchilla.

"You won't have to worry about me, buddy. I won't be here long," I whisper.

"You can understand me? Well, just don't go talking to any animal, of course. Especially animals you don't know," the chinchilla says, her tiny claws gripping the edge of the hammock as her large black eyes peek over the fabric.

Between the attempts by the raven, the deer, and the rabbit to give me advice on my first day of school, I'm fine not talking to any other animals, thank you very much.

Miss Humala drones on about MOVED, her acronym for finding density. I already know Mass Over Volume Equals Density because my science teacher at Fort Hood covered it last month. This happens to me a lot. Either I already learned what the teacher is covering or the class is five chapters ahead of where I left off at my old school.

I draw a thought bubble above Cuervito in my notebook, and he thinks, "*Moved . . . again. MOVED . . . again.*" The formula might as well be Mudándome Otra Vez Es un Desastre. Not that moving again is always a complete disaster. It's more like a tornado you know is going to make a direct hit at least every two years, uprooting and flinging you to an entirely new place against your will.

So, you know, a disaster.

I notice the kid next to me, his eyelids drooping as his pencil rolls out of his hand and across his desk. He's oblivious to the three green peas resting in his curly black hair. I hear a chuckle and a snort to my right and notice a freckled boy with a shaved head. He has four peas lined up on his desk, out of Miss Humala's sight and ready to flick at the sleeping kid.

You meet a lot of kids when you go to so many different schools. But no matter the school, the groups are the same. There's always the nose-pickers. The hyperventilating hand-raisers. The PE Olympians.

Evidently, New Haven Middle School has the pea-flickers.

I noticed this vegetable flinger when I walked into class because he had on camo pants and a patch from the Third Corps based out of Fort Hood sewn on his backpack. I started to sit by him, thinking I'd found another military kid, but then I realized that his blue tiger-stripe camo was from the Air Force and that on his backpack was a blue patch with a large red 1 on it for the First Marine Division. No one in their right mind would mix Army, Air Force, and Marine Corps. He probably got all of it at a military-surplus store.

The only thing more annoying than *actually* being a military kid is people who pretend to be military. Dad says being a soldier is a lot more than having a gun and wearing camo. He always shakes his head at men who "play soldier."

Having been the new kid five times, I've suffered my share of bullies and goons. I kick the sleeping boy's desk, and he straightens up, yawning and wiping his eyes. He looks at me through half-closed eyes, and I brush my fingers through my hair to alert him to the vegetable accessories in his hair.

He shakes his head, and the peas fall to the ground. I notice the pea-flicker scowl at me as I shrug my shoulders. The half-awake boy mumbles, "Thanks," and rests his chin on his hand. Miss Humala recites "mass over volume equals density" over and over, and his eyelids start to droop again.

From the front of the classroom, Miss Humala claps, her long red nails looking like bloody talons. "All right. Pair up and practice finding density with your partner."

I groan. A new kid's absolute favorite thing: finding a partner on the first day. Maybe Miss Humala should just go ahead and spit on me. I scan the classroom. The pea-flicker is definitely out; he's still scowling at me, his freckles fiery red meteors across his face. A girl is sitting in front of me, but she's hunched over her paper, tears dripping down onto the equations. I don't think I should bother her. Everyone else in class seems to have paired up faster than drooling high schoolers at prom.

I drum my ink-stained fingers on my desk, expecting to complete the problems by myself. Then I feel a nudge on my arm, and the drowsy boy nods at the board, asking, "You wanna?"

I shrug. We look at the six problems on the board. The kids around us scribble on their papers and argue with their partners over the right answers.

The boy takes a deep breath and says, "Whaddya get?"

I don't want to show off, but I don't need pencil and paper to figure out the problems. "Thirty-two, fifty-five point two five, and fifty-four," I say, answering the first three questions.

The boy stretches his arms above his head and

twirls his pencil in his long fingers. "Twenty-seven, seventy-two, and sixteen point five," he says, answering the second set and smirking.

I chuckle.

He leans toward my desk and looks at my sketchbook. "Wow, that's really good."

I want to tell him that I drew it from real life. And ask him if all the ravens in New Haven are this obnoxious, but I've already got being the new kid going against me. I don't need to make myself sound any weirder.

"Thanks," I reply. I add extra feathers to the legs of the raven on my page.

"New, huh?" the boy asks. "I'm Talib."

He gives a weak wave. I notice Band-Aids on three of his fingers.

"I'm Nestor," I tell him. I look around and notice that most of the class is furiously pounding buttons on their calculators. "I moved here from Fort Hood."

"You in the Army?" Talib asks as he turns his calculator upside down, attempting to write words with the numbers.

"My dad is. He's an explosive ordnance disposal specialist." Noticing Talib's raised eyebrows, I explain. "That means he disarms bombs."

"Is he . . . working right now?"

I sigh. Here it comes. "Yeah, he's in Afghanistan."

There's always an awkward silence after this. A mumbled excuse before I'm on my own again.

But Talib puts his calculator down and whispers, "Is it true that military bases have underground tunnel networks for transferring kidnapped aliens?"

"I don't think so."

"Can you buy rocket launchers at the grocery store?"

"They're usually sold out." I smirk.

"Don't kindergartners have to complete wilderness-survival training?"

"I got a blue ribbon on the tower-of-death ropes course as a six-year-old," I tell him, stifling a laugh. "The Army should hire you to write their recruitment brochures."

Talib slaps his desk and laughs, earning us a hard stare from Miss Humala.

I point to the Band-Aids wrapped around Talib's fingers and ask, "You trying to house-train a tiger?"

Talib gives a slight smile and runs his fingers through his hair. Another pea falls out, and he sighs. "Me? No, not really. My dog ran away a couple of nights ago, and I've been looking for him out in the woods. A lot of thorns are out there." He chuckles nervously and adds, "Yeah, thorns."

I'm showing Talib some of my other drawings, skipping past my Days in New Haven page, when he flinches and says, "Hey!"

He rubs the back of his neck and reveals fingers covered in butterscotch pudding.

The pea-flicker has upgraded. He cackles at Talib, showing crooked teeth under cracked lips.

Talib looks toward the front of the classroom, but Miss Humala is oblivious, hunched over a student's desk, muttering, "Mass over volume, not volume over mass! For the fifth time!"

The crying girl in front of me, Maria Carmen, I think, passes Talib a tissue and then goes back to whispering with the girl next to her. "We woke up this morning, and the goats were all gone. When I fed them last night, they were all fine. All we found were tracks leading off into the trees. I know it's still out there, just waiting to take something else. I'm never walking through the woods again," I hear Maria Carmen whisper.

She takes something out of her pocket and shows it to the girl. A bright pink tag with the number five on it.

It's the same as the tags I found in the woods, except those have a three and an eight on them. I'm still not sure what they are.

My first day of school has landed me in a tornado of weirdness.

"That's Brandon," Talib says, nodding to the pea-flicker as he wipes the pudding from the back of his neck. "I can't stand that baboon."

"Yeah, I don't think he's too high on my list, either." Maybe on a list of who I'd like to see pecked by ravens, but I don't mention that to Talib.

I close my sketchbook and feel two wet globs hit me in the cheek and forehead.

Brandon cackles and slaps his hands together. I wipe as much of the sticky pudding off my face as I can, smearing it on my blank science worksheet.

First days at a new school are about as great as finding a fingernail in your hamburger, but this pudding-throwing, pea-flicking fake soldier is making today one of my worst ever.

"Gentlemen! What exactly is going on?" Miss Humala says as she stands in front of Talib, snapping her neck to the pudding-thrower and then to me.

"War of the pudding cups," I mumble under my breath.

Miss Humala looks at me. "You'd better clean up in the bathroom," she says before marching over to Brandon. She seems more upset that I smeared pudding on her precious worksheet than the fact that it was thrown at me by a boot camp dropout in the middle of her classroom.

I scowl at Brandon's camo pants as I head for the door. He mutters, "Fire for efficiency," and sneers at me.

"It's 'fire for effect,' moron," I mutter.

What kind of messed up town has Mom dragged me to? And how can Abuela live here? Between pudding assaults, obnoxious ravens, and whatever's in the woods that has Talib and Maria Carmen freaked out, I'm feeling sorry that I corrected Mom when she took the wrong exit off the interstate. I should've just let her keep driving straight into Mexico.

CHAPTER 4

ABP. ABH.

Always Be Positive. Always Be Happy.

Mom drilled these two mantras into me about three deployments ago. It doesn't matter that I drew a complete blank today when my math teacher asked where I was from. It's not important that Mom lost half the kitchen dishes when a box fell off the moving truck on the highway. While Dad is halfway across the world, as far as he's concerned, everything is fine.

I know that when Dad is deployed, he views himself as a soldier, husband, and father, in that order. He has to so he can do his job. And Mom says we have to help Dad do his job the best he can.

But sometimes it really sucks being his last priority.

I finish my email to him, telling him about Talib and not mentioning the pudding-flicking, soldier-wannabe bully. Or that kids seem freaked out by something in the woods. As far as he knows, New Haven is a small, boring town with no annoying animals or mysterious threats lurking behind trees.

Well, half of that is true.

I close my laptop and go downstairs to Abuela's kitchen. The smell of pastelitos de guayaba fills my nostrils. My stomach reminds me that I skipped the questionable bean burritos the school cafeteria served at lunch.

"Ay, créeme. No necesitan más vinagre, chica," I hear Abuela say.

I round the corner and find Abuela in an empty kitchen.

Who was she talking to?

I grab a plate and pile three pastelitos on it. Stuffing my face with Abuela's guava pastries helps me forget my mom has moved me to a nonexistent town where bullies flick rejected dessert at you and the woods swallow up family pets. The sticky pastry crunches in my mouth as the sweet guava filling oozes out the sides.

"Who thinks your beans need more vinegar, Buela?" I ask, trying to figure out who I heard her talking to.

Abuela throws her hands in the air. "I've been making frijoles negros for years. I know how much vinegar it needs. She should stick to . . . ay, no importa."

Well, that didn't get me far.

"Oye, niño," Abuela says. "Get me a bowl for the beans."

I have no idea where Abuela keeps anything in her kitchen, so I start opening cabinet doors. In a bottom cabinet next to the fridge, I spot three small pink tags with the numbers two, seven, and nine on them.

They're the same as the tags I found in the woods and the one the girl in science class had.

Why does Abuela have these?

I finally find a bowl and hand it to Abuela. She starts to hum Celia Cruz's "Azúcar Negra," stirring a large pot of frijoles on the stove. Her slippered feet shuffle in a salsa on the floor, and she punctuates her song with a flip of her ladle every time the beans bubble up in the pot. I sit at the small kitchen table and spot a framed drawing of a rabbit holding a bunch of flowers next to the stove. Below the drawing, scrawled in blue crayon, the card reads, *Feliz día de madres. Te quiero para siempre. Tu hijo, Raulito.*

I ignore that the rabbit my dad drew looks like the result of a radioactive experiment. It's sweet that Abuela framed his Mother's Day card. I've given Mom lots of drawings over the years, but she never hangs them up. I think it's because it's just something else she would have to take down when we move again.

Mom comes in from the living room and plops down next to me at the table, deflating with a heavy sigh. She arches her back, stretching it. With all of Dad's deployments, my mom has moved our belongings all by herself five times. If she were a superhero, she'd be La Empacadora, faster than professional movers, able to leap giant packing boxes in a single bound.

I set a pastelito on a plate and slide it over to Mom. She puts her arm around me and squeezes my shoulder.

"You know your dad doesn't like guava?" she says, once again rubbing her thumb over Dad's wedding ring hanging from her neck. "That man is crazy. At least I know you'll put your dish in the dishwasher once you're done. Unlike him."

"He's not that messy," I say, shaking my head.

"Hah! Not that messy. You'd think a military man would be better at making the bed or folding clothes."

I look at Abuela, and she gives Mom a sympathetic smile.

I press the pastry crumbs on my plate with my finger. Mom does this every deployment. She always goes through a phase where she complains about Dad. It makes it sound like she's mad at him, but I know the truth. Sometimes it hurts too much missing somebody, so you try to convince yourself you don't really need them. And you think that trying not to love them so much makes it hurt less when they're gone.

It usually doesn't work.

"And your first day? How was it?" Abuela asks, changing the subject.

"Pretty much the same as the nine others I've had," I lie. Though this was definitely the first time I got smacked in the face with pudding. How many points do I get for that?

Mom looks at me, tilting her head in confusion. "Ten first days? Has it really been that many?"

I push my plate away from me. "Yep. And this time it wasn't even the military's fault. You and Dad decided to move when we didn't even have to."

Abuela's shoulders slump, and I regret my words immediately. I'm glad we're living with her. I'm glad Mom and Dad decided we could live with Abuela instead of living on post. I just don't think my parents get how much it stinks always having to start over.

"Well," Mom says, brushing crumbs off her hands, "let's take a tenth first-day selfie for your dad. I bet you earned a thousand points for my challenge."

I don't bother to correct her and say it was more like negative fifty points.

Mom pulls her phone from her back pocket, and we snap a picture. She tries to get the pastelitos in the shot, too, but ends up cutting off our heads at the nose. It's just our crumb-covered mouths and guava pastries.

I clear my throat. "Buela, are there lots of animals in the woods behind your house? You know . . . like, scary ones?" I chuckle nervously.

Mom looks up from her phone. "Aren't you a little old to be scared of animals? I thought twelve-year-olds weren't afraid of anything."

"No, it's just that some kids at school were talking

about the woods. This one kid lost his dog, and this other girl lost . . . goats, I think?"

Abuela's breath catches in her throat, and she coughs.

Mom's eyebrow rises. "Goats?"

"Cariño, this is Texas," Abuela says, waving her ladle toward the backyard. "My hairdresser, he carries a hunting rifle to the grocery store. And the bank? The bank raffled off a shotgun to a nine-year-old. There are definitely no animales locos in the woods. They would've been completely destroyed. Ya tú sabes." She smacks her hands together.

Mom puts her hand on my back. "You don't think they were just making up stories for the new kid, do you? You know, like in Kentucky?"

I shrug. Talib actually seemed nice. "I hope not."

Before Mom can respond, there's a sharp knock on the back door. Abuela shuffles over to answer it.

The crying girl from science class, Maria Carmen, is standing on our porch. "Does Nestor live here? You know, the pudding boy?"

"Pudding boy? I've been in town exactly three days and I already have a nickname?" I mutter under my breath.

"Who?" Mom looks at me, confused.

Abuela moves aside and motions Maria Carmen into the house, winking at me. Maria Carmen's inky black hair is in six braids down the back of her head. Her eyes aren't a watery red anymore, so I guess she stopped crying.

"You should join the trivia club. It meets in Miss Humala's room during lunch." She smacks a flyer down on the table. It's covered in neat handwriting, and the border is decorated with drawings of lions, sharks, eagles, and llamas. They're not too bad.

A smile grows along the side of Abuela's mouth. I don't like the way Mom keeps looking from Maria Carmen to me and then to Abuela, smirking.

I stare down at my empty plate, unable to distract myself with food. "Why do you think I should be in a trivia club?"

Maria Carmen smooths one of her braids with the palm of her hand. "Because in science today, you correctly answered all of Miss Humala's questions under your breath. I heard you."

Busted.

Mom looks at me and shakes her head. "He never participates. All his teachers say so."

Yeah, Mom, I don't. Waving my hand wildly in the air kind of ruins the whole "under the radar" thing I've got going on.

Maria Carmen puts her hands on her hips, tapping her foot. "Well, are you going to join?"

Mom nudges me. "You should join, Nestor. You and your dad are always quizzing each other." She turns to Maria Carmen. "They're always quizzing each other."

We get it, Mom. The problem with being an only child with a deployed dad is that your mom gets to focus all her attention on you.

"I think it's decided. You join," Abuela says, pointing at me with her ladle. The look on her face tells me this isn't up for debate.

Mom kisses my forehead and gets up from the table. "That's wonderful," she says. "I've got to run. Don't want to be late for my first day!"

Mom heads out of the house, dressed in light blue scrubs. She's an intensive care nurse at the hospital in Springdale, a few towns over. She always had a nursing job on post, so this is her first time traveling for work. I'm sure she's going to take a selfie for Dad in front of her new hospital.

"So you don't usually join things, I guess?" Maria

Carmen asks as Abuela hands her a plate with two pastelitos and pulls out a chair for her.

I shrug. "Not really. Not since I joined a soccer team when we lived at Fort Lewis in Washington."

"What happened?"

"I practiced for hours, kicking the ball against the side of our house. Drove my mom nuts. I watched soccer drills on YouTube every night."

"And?"

"We moved before my first game."

Maria Carmen gives me a sympathetic smile. "Well, look at it this way. Trivia club will give you a break from Brandon."

Abuela turns from the boiling pot of black beans on the stove. "Who is this Brandon?"

I glare at Maria Carmen and shake my head. Abuela doesn't need to know about the pudding-thrower. "No one, Buela. Just a kid at school."

"Por supuesto, no one. I'm sure," Abuela mumbles as she sits down with us.

"Thanks for the pastelitos, Señora Lopez. You make the best ones I've ever had."

Abuela beams with pride and squeezes Maria

Carmen's hand. "Don't worry, niña. They'll find out what happened to your goats. It'll be okay."

Maria Carmen lowers her head. "I know. Thanks."

She takes out a pink tag from her pocket and sets it on the table. "I just wish we could figure out what took them."

Abuela doesn't respond, so I point to the tag and ask, "What is that?"

Maria Carmen rubs her thumb over the tag. "It's an ear tag. We put them on our goats to keep track of them."

I don't tell Maria Carmen that I found two of them in the woods. She seems scared enough already of what might be out there. And I definitely don't tell her that Abuela has three more tags in her cabinet.

Suddenly, Maria Carmen pushes back from the table and stands. "I . . . I have to go."

Abuela and I follow her to the door. She turns and says to Abuela, "Please don't tell my mom I was here."

I give them both a puzzled look, but they don't clarify.

I step outside and watch Maria Carmen disappear up our street, wondering about goats and why her mother wouldn't want her at our house.

Cuervito, perched in a tree in the yard, screeches above me. "So you survived the first day! And you already got a girlfriend!"

He hops up and down on the branch. "Things are looking up for you, kid," he squawks.

I consider giving him a rude gesture but change my mind.

"You'd better go away," I whisper, worried Abuela will hear me outside arguing with the local wildlife. "There's only so many annoying raven comments I can take."

Cuervito screeches and beats his wings, the sound thudding through the evening air. "But your abuela said . . . ! Well, never mind."

I stomp my foot on the ground. "What did she say?"

Cuervito ignores me and dives down, pecking at one of Abuela's tomatoes. He sails off into the night, but not before pooping on the garden gnome.

I turn back into the house and set the table for dinner by myself. As I put down a second plate, a noise in the backyard catches my attention. I look out the window and spot Abuela. She's marching off into the woods, a large kitchen knife in her hand.

CHAPTER 5

THE FIRST ANIMAL I EVER HEARD SPEAK was a black-and-white guinea pig named Mrs. Pancake. She lived in a large blue cage at the day care Mom took me to while she worked at a hospital at Fort Benning, Georgia. I fed Mrs. Pancake my unwanted Goldfish crackers and stale pretzel rods.

"Keep 'em coming, kid. Keep 'em coming," Mrs. Pancake said, rocking on her back and rubbing her swollen, furry belly.

The first time the guinea pig spoke to me, I thought I was just imagining it. I had a pretty hyperactive imagination then. But this guinea pig looked straight at me and struck a deal. "You keep me nose-deep in snacks, and I'll poop on the toy-hogging snot over there who keeps biting you."

So at four years old, I realized I could hear animals talk and immediately started a business as a toddler snack-stealer.

I never told my parents about it. My dad is thousands of miles away, dodging bullets and bombs. My mom is worried about my dad, thousands of miles away, dodging bullets and bombs. They don't need a freak kid to worry about, too.

Of all the animals I've talked to, though, none has ever prepared me for the sight of my abuela stomping off into the dark woods with a knife. She didn't come back to the house until after I went to bed, and I was too scared to ask her about it in the morning.

I sit in science class, sketching a picture of Abuela fighting a zombie deer with a large wooden spoon, her purple hair flying in the wind as she jabs at the deer's glowing red eyes. Miss Humala drones on. She's still reviewing how to find density since most of the class failed her pop quiz. Her abnormally long neck juts forward each time she says *volume*. Maria Carmen sits in front of me, squinting at the fluorescent lights hanging from the ceiling as she flips her braids over her shoulder. Talib leans his head on his hand next to me, playing tic-tac-toe with himself on his paper. I'm not sure how that works.

To my right, I hear Brandon, the camo-wearing bully, whisper to a kid next to him, "Dad and I shot a deer yesterday. Big ol' doe."

I worry about the white-tailed deer I drew in the woods yesterday and decided to call Chela. I know for a fact that deer season doesn't start for two weeks. So Brandon isn't just a military wannabe; he's a bad hunter, too.

Miss Humala claps and says, "Before we continue, Principal Jelani has asked all the teachers to make an announcement. Students are not to walk through the woods before or after school. Make sure you take the roads through town to get home."

She narrows her eyes and scans the room. "I strongly recommend that you follow Principal Jelani's instructions. We've had too many strange animal disappearances in town, and we don't know what's in the woods. So best to just stay away."

The students around me start to murmur. I look at

Maria Carmen. She flips the pink goat tag between her fingers and then shoves it into her pocket. Talib sighs next to me.

"I guess I won't figure out what happened to my dog. But I don't really want to get eaten out there, either. So good call," he says.

The glint from Abuela's knife flashes in my brain. At least if no one else is supposed to be out there, they won't see her stomping around doing . . . whatever it is she's doing.

Miss Humala clears her throat and starts to divide the class between those who failed her pop quiz (pretty much the entire class) and those who passed (me, Talib, and Maria Carmen).

Miss Humala gives us free time while she drills "mass over volume equals density" over and over to the rest of the class. Talib points to a cabinet near Milla the chinchilla's cage and whispers, "She has games in there that we can play."

I open the cabinet and scan the worn boxes and games, which look like they probably belonged to Miss Humala's great-grandmother.

"Nice job on the quiz, kiddo," Milla says, scampering

up her cage and diving into her hammock. "But that doesn't mean you can pet me. Nope. No touching."

"I hadn't planned on it," I whisper to her.

Finally, I see exactly the game I want to play with Talib and Maria Carmen—a plastic bag filled with dominoes.

Maria Carmen, Talib, and I push our desks together, and I dump the dominoes out of the bag. They clatter on the fake-wood desktops, and several jealous eyes turn to stare at us.

"Maybe a little less enthusiasm," Miss Humala says, clearing her throat and taking a break from pounding her fist on the formula written on the board.

Talib chuckles. "I don't think she's gonna be cool with us lining these up and knocking them down."

I shake my head. "Nope. I'm going to teach you guys *actual* dominoes."

I slide ten tiles to each of us and explain the rules of the game.

"Where'd you learn to play?" Maria Carmen asks, lining up her tiles in front of her so Talib and I can't see them.

"From my abuelo. Each time we moved somewhere

new, he traveled to see me so we could play dominoes in our new kitchen," I explain.

I scan the dominoes and hold up a double-nine tile. "This is the caja de muertos, the dead man's box."

Talib takes the tile from me. "I like that."

"And this is the caja de dientes, the box of teeth," I say, showing them a double-six tile.

"Your abuelo taught you all this?" Maria Carmen asks.

"Yeah. And when I was little, I learned a new Spanish curse word every time I beat him."

Talib hands me the caja de muertos. "You have to teach me those."

He sets up three of his dominoes in a line and knocks them over in a cascade. "So why'd you move to New Haven?"

"My dad grew up here. My mom and I are staying with my abuela while my dad's in Afghanistan. My mom thought it would be nice staying with family instead of on an Army base."

Talib nods and sets up his dominoes in a line again to tip over. "How many places have you lived?"

"New Haven makes six," I tell them. "Never been a Fighting Armadillo, though."

"I wouldn't get your hopes up," Maria Carmen says, rolling her eyes. "Our football team is so small that the same kids have to play offense and defense. They're usually so tired by the last quarter they just lie down on the field and let the other team run over them."

Talib nods and twirls a tile between his fingers. "Did you always go to school on a military base?"

"Yep."

"What was your mascot at your last school? The Parachuting Penguins? Bayoneting Beavers?"

I smile. "No, we were the General Sherman School of Tanks and Missiles Valiant Vultures."

Maria Carmen and Talib stare at me with wide eyes.

"Kidding."

"You've really gone to six schools? I've only ever lived in New Haven," Maria Carmen says. "We drove up to Dallas once to visit my tía Maricela, but that's the farthest I've ever been."

"We went on vacation to Florida a couple of years ago. But other than that, my butt has been in New Haven," Talib says.

I lay down the first tile, and we start taking turns matching up the numbers on each tile. I shake my head, thinking about how Maria Carmen and Talib have always been here. They've always known where their home is. Always *had* a home.

I can't even imagine what that's like. Must be nice.

Talib spins a tile between his thumb and forefinger, plotting his next move. "So where have you lived?"

I list all the places the Lopez family has moved boxes. "I was born at Fort Benning, Georgia. Then we moved to Fort Carson, Colorado. We stayed there until I was in second grade. Next, we moved to Fort Lewis, Washington, for a little bit and then Fort Campbell, Kentucky. After that was Fort Hood just north of here, and finally"—I drum my fingers on my desk in finale—"New Haven."

I get tired just thinking of all the places I've kicked packing boxes under my bed.

"That is so cool," Maria Carmen says, slapping down a double-four tile. "I would kill to get to travel so much."

"No kidding. You've seen the ocean, right? Like not just the Gulf of Mexico, but the actual ocean?" Talib leans forward, scanning the tiles we've laid down, searching for a match.

I picture the wide Pacific Ocean when we were stationed in Washington, the waves glistening like diamonds as the sun dipped below the horizon. I'd fall asleep right on the beach, the lullaby of the waves lapping the shore as Mom would run her fingers through my hair.

I still don't think moving so much is a good thing. But Maria Carmen and Talib are right—I *have* seen a lot of the country.

I just haven't seen a lot of my dad.

CHAPTER 6

DON'T GO IN THE DARK, musty basement with creaking stairs and flickering lights. Don't answer the phone when you're home alone and the caller ID says AX MURDERER. Don't enter the decaying, abandoned building covered in suffocating vines and bloody handprints.

I've seen enough horror movies to know what you are and aren't supposed to do if you want to survive.

Don't walk through the woods in your town when you've seen your abuela stomp off into the trees with a knife.

I guess Talib and I aren't that smart.

After hearing Brandon brag about shooting a deer with his dad, I wanted to check on Chela, the doe I met yesterday. Even though Miss Humala told us to stay out of the woods. When Talib saw me take off into the trees after school, he tagged along, saying I shouldn't go alone.

As we tromp down the path, I notice Talib's dark eyes dart around every live oak tree and scan every rocky hill, searching for some unknown threat ready to devour us whole.

Talib picks up an acorn and launches it at a tree trunk. He misses by a foot. The acorn bounces down the trail ahead of us, scaring lizards and squirrels, who scamper under fallen leaves and branches. "So is your dad really strict about keeping your room neat and making your bed since he's in the military?"

I laugh. "I have a Cuban mom and a Cuban grandma. The military is nothing compared with them when it comes to keeping a house clean."

I can hear the sound of Mom's clicking tongue as she juts out her chin, pointing to the dirty clothes on my floor or my unmade bed. Nothing makes me clean faster than her raised eyebrow. And now she has Abuela as reinforcement when she's not home.

Talib shakes his head. "Sounds like my mom. So how long has your dad been away?" he asks, kicking a rock across our path.

I could give him the exact number of days right now. Along with a Days in New Haven page, I have a Days Dad's Been Gone page in my sketchbook. It has 104 marks.

"He's been downrange a little over three months," I tell him, shoving my hands into my pockets.

"Downrange?"

"Deployed. Overseas." I'm not sure why I said *downrange*. I've never liked that term. It always makes me think of shooting ranges. Downrange is where the bullets land. It's where Dad is.

Wanting to change the subject, I ask, "Are you looking for something out here? It seems like you are."

Talib stops in his tracks. "I, uh, I was hoping to find my dog, George."

"Your dog's name is George?"

"Yeah, he disappeared last week. I've been looking for him." Talib's eyes dart to a cedar tree with three long, jagged marks on it. His eyes grow wide, and he draws in a sharp breath. They look like scratches from a claw.

"You think your dog might be running around the woods?"

Talib scuffs his foot in the dirt. "Well, no, not anymore, I don't think."

This isn't making much sense, but Talib doesn't seem to want to say more about George's mysterious disappearance.

I continue down the trail, and my stomach growls in protest. "Let's keep going, man. I'm hungry," I tell Talib. He follows me, but only after glancing at the claw-marked tree trunk one last time.

We pass the spot where I sketched Chela yesterday, though she's nowhere to be found. I stop and scan the hills around us, noticing a glint under a mesquite bush. I hurry over and see the blade of a large kitchen knife plunged into the root of the bush. Small bits of thin white paper surround the knife.

I look closer and realize it's not paper.

It's snakeskin.

Kicking dirt over the shed skin, I stand in front of the knife as Talib approaches.

"I thought we were gonna keep going," he says, his voice shaky. He pushes on my arm to urge me forward.

"What are you so scared of? I'm sorry your dog is gone, but what's the deal?" Between the knife, the claw mark, and the snakeskin, I'm beginning to suspect there's plenty to be scared of in these woods. But I don't want Talib to think my abuela has anything to do with it.

Talib wipes his nose with the back of his hand. "I went looking for George out here a couple of nights ago. And I saw something."

"Dude, what did you see?"

Talib stands there and stares at me, his mouth mutely opening and closing, trying to find the words.

"Well, I found George's collar by a big cactus, and when I went to pick it up, I heard growling. I thought maybe it was him, even though George doesn't really growl like that. I saw this big, furry brown thing with huge teeth and claws. It was absolutely, most definitely not a dog." Talib's eyebrows rise. "But then it changed."

I shake my head, unsure if I heard Talib correctly. "It *what*?"

Before he can explain, I hear a shout and a cry.

Talib opens his mouth to speak, but I'm not paying attention anymore. The cries grow louder, echoing over the hills.

"Help! Help!"

I look at Talib. "Do you hear that?"

"What? The howling?"

"No. Somebody's calling for help."

Talib scrunches his eyebrows at me, but I take off running toward the sound.

"Help! Please help!" The cries pierce my ears.

Talib follows me, breathing hard. We crest the top of a hill and spot a figure below us, writhing in the dirt next to a large century cactus.

It's a coyote.

The small reddish animal tries to stand, but his back leg is caught in a clamp of interlocked, large metal teeth. With each strain against the round clamp, the coyote yelps and stumbles on the ground.

"What is that?" Talib asks.

I shake my head. "It's a hunting trap. It must've snapped around that coyote's leg the second he stepped on it."

Talib winces. "That doesn't seem right."

"It's not. Hunters use them to trap animals,

sometimes predators they want off their land, sometimes animals they're hunting for fur. Dad says they're
cruel. An animal can stay trapped for days in it and
starve to death."

"Please help me. Please!" the coyote cries, saliva
frothing at the corners of his mouth.

I run over and kneel down next to the injured animal. The coyote bares his teeth and growls, not knowing if I'm a friend or foe.

I raise my hands. "It's okay; I'm not here to hurt
you. I'm going to help you."

"You can understand me?" the coyote asks.

"Yes, I can," I tell him.

"Yes, you can what?" Talib asks behind me.

"Nothing," I say, shaking my head. One problem at
a time.

"What are you going to do, Nestor?" Talib asks,
coming closer and kneeling down next to me.

"We need to release the trap from around his leg."

Talib examines the trap. It's a half circle of sharp
metal teeth folded together. "This is one of Brandon's.
I'm sure of it. He and his dad aren't exactly known for
their legal hunting methods."

I clench my hands into fists. This Brandon kid is

steadily rising on my list of people I'd like to see rocketed to the surface of Mars. *Without* a space suit.

I keep my hands on the coyote, rubbing his fur and reassuring him that he'll be okay. His body is warm and rises up and down as he pants. Talib presses two round tabs on either end of the trap, and it snaps open with a click.

"It's okay, buddy. You're free," I tell the coyote as he lets out a soft yelp. He tries to stand on his back leg, but his small body falls into the dirt.

"I can't walk. It hurts too much."

"Okay, let me carry you. Will that be all right?"

Behind me, I hear Talib clear his throat. "Nestor, are you talking to that coyote?"

I ignore his question. I'm not sure how I would answer it anyway. I'm not ready yet. Talib seems like a good guy, but I don't want to send him screaming by revealing my secret.

Picking up the coyote in my arms, I'm careful not to put pressure on his back leg. Talib and I continue down the trail with the injured animal.

"I can't believe he's letting you carry him," Talib says.

"I must have a way with animals," I tell him.

The coyote shudders in my arms. "Somebody's not telling the truth," he says.

"Shush," I whisper, scratching behind his ear with my finger.

Talib and I pass a thick patch of mesquite trees when we hear stomping along the trail behind us.

We turn and see Brandon, his face red and his fists clenched.

"That coyote's mine, you thieves," he snarls, kicking dirt at us with his untied shoe.

"Traps are illegal in these woods, you moron," I snap back. I haven't lived in New Haven long, but Dad always makes sure I know the rules wherever we go.

Brandon rushes toward me, eyes on fire. His feet skid in the dirt inches from us. He leans forward, his nose almost touching mine. His hot breath blows in my face. I smell traces of the rubbery chicken fingers served in the cafeteria today.

Out of the corner of my eye, I see Talib bend down and pick up a rock.

"That animal should've stayed in the trap," Brandon hisses, poking me in the chest with his finger.

The coyote in my arms raises his head and clamps his small, sharp teeth around Brandon's finger.

Brandon screams and draws his bloody index finger back, wrapping his other hand around it. He huffs and stomps away from us, shouting over his shoulder, "This isn't over!"

I look at Talib, whose fingers are still clenched tight around the rock. His chest heaves up and down.

"What were you planning to do with that?"

Talib looks down at his hand. "I don't know. Maybe juggle to distract him?"

I chuckle. "C'mon, let's go."

We head toward our houses, and the coyote snuggles in close to my body. The sun starts to dip below the tree line, sending snaking shadows across our path.

Talib walks behind me, flinging his rock into the mesquite bushes. "Um, Nestor, what exactly are you planning to do with that coyote?"

I think for a moment, considering my options. "Do you think my abuela would be okay with a new pet?" I ask.

Talib laughs and slaps my back. "Sure, buddy. I'll bring flowers to your funeral. You like roses or tulips?"

He takes off toward his house, just a block away from mine, and I keep going until I see the blue paint of Abuela's house. As I walk closer, the coyote raises his head and mumbles, "Don't let her get me."

I look down at his trembling body. "Don't you mean *him*?"

The coyote presses into my chest, and I feel his pounding heartbeat. "No, *her*. Don't let the witch get me."

CHAPTER 7

Hey Dad,

You know, I was afraid that Abuela lived in the most boring town on the planet, but I was wrong. The woods are a minefield of hunting traps. There's a kid at school who likes to poke his long, unclipped nails into my chest. I have a coyote sleeping under my bed who swears he was attacked by a witch. Oh, and did I mention I saw Abuela stomp off into the woods carrying a knife?

I scratch through everything I've written and turn to a clean page in my sketchbook.

Always Be Positive.

Always Be Happy.

Hi, Dad!

So Abuela's town isn't that bad. There are some pretty cool animals here. You can even see them up close! I joined the trivia club. I know, can you believe I actually joined something? You'd be proud. I've got two friends in the club, Talib and Maria Carmen.

By the way, the answer to your question about what type of sheep in Afghanistan is named after a famous explorer is ... Marco Polo sheep! Now here's one for you. This animal is known for howling at the moon to communicate and has even been known to adapt its habitat to cities. Think hard!

Hope you're doing okay. Love you. Stay safe.
                                                    Nestor

I close my sketchbook, planning to mail Dad's letter when I get home after school.

I take my fork and poke at the gray glob on my red plastic tray.

Miss Humala clears her throat and raises an eyebrow. "That doesn't look too appetizing, does it?"

I pause, my fork hovered over the cafeteria tuna surprise, which I've learned is the same at every school. The surprise is it's not tuna. I've sat through several days of science class with Miss Humala barking orders and glaring death rays into students' skulls. Maria Carmen and Talib said she was nice in the first few weeks of school, always stashing bags of peppermints in her desk to toss to students when they answered correctly. But about three weeks ago, the stress of attempting to teach science to incompetent twelve-year-olds must've gotten to her.

When I arrived in her classroom for trivia club practice, Miss Humala was sitting at her desk, a stack of papers in front of her. She hovered a red pen over one paper, a look of malicious glee in her eyes.

I'm not sure there's anything more awkward than sitting in a teacher's classroom by yourself.

Maybe coming to school naked; that's a close second.

"So how are you liking your new school, Nestor?" Miss Humala asks.

Please, no small talk, I want to say. Just let me sit here not eating my tuna surprise. She doesn't need to bother getting to know me. I'll be gone in a few months anyway.

I stick my fork in the inedible mass on my tray. "It's fine," I mumble.

Miss Humala looks at me with her large brown eyes. She spins her red pen between her fingers. "You know, I'm kind of a new kid here myself. This is only my second year in New Haven."

I nod. I'm used to teachers trying to connect. But I've never had a teacher who really got what it was like to move so much. So at least she's trying.

"Why'd you move to New Haven?" I ask her.

"Um, I think I needed a fresh start." She bites her lip and sets down her red pen. "Sometimes you just have to get away from things."

A thud at the door keeps me from asking Miss Humala what she was running from. Maria Carmen drags Talib by the arm into the classroom and deposits him into the seat next to me. She takes the seat on my other side and flips her braids over her shoulders.

Miss Humala looks at us and claps twice. She grabs a stack of cards from a drawer in her desk. "Let's begin, shall we? We've got a lot of practice ahead of us if we're going to make it to finals. I'm optimistic about you bunch."

"When are finals?" Talib asks.

"The end of May," Maria Carmen responds.

I pull my sketchbook out of my backpack and flip to my Days in New Haven page. I wonder if I'll be able to make marks all the way through May. That's seven months away. I look at Talib and Maria Carmen. Maria Carmen twirls a braid around her finger as Talib yawns and stretches his T-shirt over his belly. I've made some interesting friends here.

Friends.

I shove my hands into my pockets and lower my head. I should know better than to make friends so quickly. If moving to so many schools has taught me anything, it's that the fewer people you bring close, the fewer you have to awkwardly hug and say good-bye to. And the fewer who promise to write and then never do.

When I was in second grade, I was friends with Steven Linner. We made up a secret code that we used to write notes to each other. Then Dad announced we were moving to Fort Lewis, and Steven and I promised we'd keep writing to each other in our secret code. I went to the mailbox every day once we were in Washington, but no letter ever came. Eventually, I stopped trying to write to him.

Watching Maria Carmen and Talib, I wonder if we'll make those same false promises in a few months.

Miss Humala stands in front of her desk and holds out the first card. "This animal is a type of worm that drinks three to four times its body weight in blood." She clicks her large front teeth expectantly.

"What's a leech?" Talib says as he raises his head from his desk and rubs his eyes.

"Correct!" she cries, stomping her foot on the floor.

Talib looks at me and grins. "This is better than being pudding targets in the cafeteria, right?"

"I guess. And I don't think she would've taken no for an answer." I point to Maria Carmen.

As if she heard me, she passes Talib and I each a stack of index cards and a bell. "These are your study cards. You should staple them together by animal genus. And ring your bell when you know the answer. See if you can beat me," she says, winking.

While Miss Humala continues quizzing us, Talib and I sort our cards into groups of closely related animals.

I learn that this is the second year New Haven Middle School has had a trivia club. That Miss Humala started it when she was a new teacher last year. It was mostly eighth graders who traded in-school suspension for involvement in a club, and they answered only two questions right their first competition. The club disbanded before the end of the school year, when two of the members duct-taped bottle rockets to their opponents' chairs and superglued the moderator's hand to his microphone.

"This bird can sleep while it flies." Miss Humala stretches her long neck and taps the quiz card on her desk.

I'd love to say I know this answer because I read it in a book. But you tend to remember when a bird flies over your head and you hear it *snoring*.

I ring the bell on my desk. "Albatross!"

We'd been stationed at Fort Lewis in Washington two months before my mom and I visited the coast.

While we were there, I saw a white bird with enormous wings soaring above me, snoring and muttering to herself, "Just five more minutes, Mom."

Miss Humala continues with her cards, and Maria Carmen beats me to a correct answer three times. I need to step up my game.

Talib leans toward me and whispers, "How's the coyote? Your abuela excited about the new family pet?"

I wait to answer him until Maria Carmen shouts out another correct answer.

"I wrapped his leg. He's sleeping under my bed right now."

Talib shakes his head. "If your abuela finds it, you might be coming home to coyote stew for dinner."

Miss Humala clears her throat, and Talib and I straighten up. She pulls another card from the stack on her desk. Her eyebrows rise as a smile creeps across her lips.

"This mammal is known as a scaly anteater and is covered in hard, platelike scales."

I close my eyes, searching my brain for the right answer.

Maria Carmen rings the bell on her desk. "Armadillo."

Talib lets out a laugh and slams his hand down on the bell on his desk. "Nope. It's a pangolin." When Miss Humala gives him a thumbs-up, Maria Carmen glares at him and slides his bell farther from his reach.

"Excellent!" Miss Humala claps, her white-blond curly hair bouncing up and down. "You all really have a knack for this."

Each year, the regional quiz bowl picks a focus category for sixth graders. This year it's zoology. I feel good about my chances but don't bother to suggest I might have an unfair advantage.

Miss Humala clears her throat and continues. "This nocturnal African animal eats ants and termites and is best known for being at the start of the dictionary."

Before Maria Carmen, Talib, or I can answer, the door to Miss Humala's classroom bangs open.

Brandon barges in and slumps down in a seat at the back of the classroom. He's wearing an oversize fatigue-green jacket with patches from the Army, Air Force, and Marine Corps crudely sewn all over it.

Miss Humala purses her lips. "You're late, Brandon. Practice starts promptly at the beginning of lunch."

Brandon rolls his eyes and mumbles, "Whatever," under his breath. He shoves his hands into his pockets, but not before I notice a white bandage wrapped around his index finger.

I'm going to buy that coyote some treats.

I tap Maria Carmen on the shoulder. "Are you kidding me?" I whisper. "You recruited him, too?"

Maria Carmen shakes her head. "No way. It was Miss Humala. She's making him do it to help his grade."

Fantastic.

I look back at Brandon. He's wearing hunting-camo pants and twirling a rabbit's foot key chain between his fingers.

"Shot it myself," he sneers at me.

I roll my eyes.

Miss Humala selects another card and holds it up in front of her nose. "This primate barks and screams when angry and will even throw its own—"

A knock on the door interrupts her question. Miss

Leander, our math teacher, motions Miss Humala over.

While they talk, Brandon flicks a wadded-up piece of paper at Talib.

"Look at me," he says. "A regular Carlos Hancock."

I throw my hands up. Brandon really doesn't know military trivia. Carlos *Hathcock* was a Marine Corps sniper from the Vietnam War. Before Dad's first deployment, I told him I was worried about his being safe. He ruffled my hair and said, "Don't worry, buddy. I've got a bunch of Carlos Hathcocks watching over me."

"You've got to be kidding me," I say, glaring at Brandon. "It's Carlos *Hath*cock. Don't you know anything?"

Brandon's mouth drops open. He narrows his eyes at me. "What are you, some kind of military genius?"

"His dad's in the Army," Talib says before I can respond. "He's in Afghanistan."

Brandon's top lip curls into a sneer. "You'd better hope he doesn't get blown up over there."

A rock drops in my gut, and my cheeks burn. I

clench my fists and push up from my chair. Before I can get to Brandon, Maria Carmen jumps up.

"Here are your study cards!" she exclaims, her voice quivering with nerves.

I sit back down as she hands Brandon a stack of index cards. He shoves them into the pocket of his pants.

Maria Carmen puts her hand on my shoulder and gives me a sympathetic smile as she sits back down. My fingernails are still digging into my palms, and I can't slow down my breathing.

Miss Humala comes back to her post at the front of the classroom. I don't hear the rest of her practice questions, my ears still burning with anger.

When lunch is over, we stay in Miss Humala's room for science class. Maria Carmen keeps her head lowered, and I can't look at Brandon without clenching my fists. When class is finally done, Brandon slumps out of the classroom ahead of us. Talib, Maria Carmen, and I head down the hall to our next class, and I put my hand on Maria Carmen's arm. "Thanks," I tell her. "I was about to punch Brandon's nose into the back of his skull."

Maria Carmen shrugs. "He shouldn't have said what he did. It isn't right."

Tears well in her eyes, and her bottom lip quivers. She rushes away from us, down the hall, a blur of swinging black braids.

"Did I say something wrong?" I ask Talib.

He looks at me and shakes his head. "It wasn't you. Her brother was killed in Iraq two years ago."

CHAPTER 8

DAD SAYS A GOOD PERSON doesn't react in anger. He told me this when I was nine and fell off my skateboard, skinning both knees. I kicked my skateboard into a storm drain in front of our house on post in Kentucky and shouted a couple of words I learned from Abuelo.

I know Dad would be disappointed that I almost punched Brandon.

But now Brandon has me pushed up against the wall outside the gym, my shoulder blades digging into the hard bricks. My forearms burn as I clench my fists.

Just one punch to get his freckle- and zit-spattered skin away from my face. Dad would never know. He's thousands of miles away.

"Stay away from my traps," Brandon hisses, his knuckles white around the sleeves of my T-shirt.

I take a deep breath, the air burning my stretching lungs, and put my hands up in surrender.

Dad won't know if I rearrange the line of Brandon's nose, but I can still feel his hand on my shoulder, his calm, patient voice in my ear. The emptiness of his absence matching the fullness of the memories.

Brandon lets go and stomps away. The curious students who surrounded us meander away, occupied by the next joke or drama.

Talib and Maria Carmen rush toward me. "You okay?" Talib asks.

I brush my hands on my jeans. "Yeah. Bullies like him aren't really anything new."

Talib looks from Maria Carmen to me and sighs. "Well, this has been a completely awful day. Let's go home."

Maria Carmen nods, biting her lip.

"Through the woods," I tell them and hike my backpack onto my shoulder.

Talib shakes his head. "You want to shove this day even farther down the toilet?"

I fix a hard look on Maria Carmen and Talib. "I don't care what the school says. I'm getting rid of every one of Brandon's traps."

Maria Carmen raises her head, her voice full for the first time since she ran down the hall. "Sounds good to me."

We head off into the woods and spread out a little on the trail. I scan each rock and search the base of every tree, looking for metal circles with sharp teeth. But I'm doing it only half-heartedly, my mind still swirling from Brandon's black words during trivia club practice.

I catch up to Maria Carmen on the trail and clear my throat. "I'm sorry about your brother," I tell her, my voice a whisper catching in the breeze and floating through the trees.

She lowers her head and sighs. "Thanks. I figured Talib would tell you."

The three of us walk in silence, past tall cacti and rambling live oak branches. Cuervito soars above us but doesn't say a single obnoxious word. Even he knows now's not the time.

Maria Carmen breaks our silence so softly I almost don't hear her at first. "I miss him," she says.

Talib and I look at each other and nod. Maria Carmen picks a leaf from an oak tree and presses it between her fingers.

"He was a military policeman in Iraq. His Humvee convoy had been warned about people dangling grenades from the tops of overpasses with fishing line, waiting for the soldiers to drive under and hit them."

I close my eyes. I don't want to hear this. I want to picture Maria Carmen at the skate park with her brother, laughing and daring each other to attempt new tricks. I want to see her brother cheering and pumping his fists as Maria Carmen graduates from high school. I don't want to hear about the dark threat that devoured him.

The same threat that stalks my dad.

But I owe it to Maria Carmen to listen.

Maria Carmen stops on the trail and brushes a tear from her eye. "They were out for a morning patrol through Baghdad. He was the top gunner in the Humvee. And he didn't see it."

Talib puts his hand on Maria Carmen's shoulder. I grab her trembling hand and squeeze it. We stand together on the trail as Cuervito flies in a circle above us, a sentry to our vigil.

"He wasn't even regular Army. Just National Guard. All he wanted was to be able to go to college." Maria Carmen sighs and raises her head. "I miss him so much."

Bullies and traps are forgotten. We march home in silence. Maria Carmen breaks off from our group first, and then a few minutes later, Talib heads off toward his house.

Gray clouds surround me as I enter Abuela's house. Tossing my backpack onto the living room couch, I mutter, "Buela, I'm home."

I hear her in the dining room, her sewing machine whirring.

"Oye, this doesn't need sequins. Dejame en paz!"

I meander into the dining room, rubbing my thumb on the notch in the doorway that marks Dad's height when he was my age. I figure Abuela is talking to herself again as she runs the hem of Mom's nursing scrubs through her sewing machine set up on the table.

The day still heavy on my shoulders, I slump down into a chair and watch Abuela sew. The rhythmic whir of the machine pulls me deep into my thoughts. I have only ten marks on my Days in New Haven page, and I've already grown closer to Talib and Maria Carmen than I have to anyone my own age. I've joined a club at school, something I rarely bothered doing before since I knew I couldn't guarantee I'd be there for the whole year.

I pull at the hem of my shirt and crumple it in my hands.

Abuela looks at me over the top of her glasses, which she always wears when she sews. "You know, that's why I have to keep sewing your mami's nursing scrubs," she says, indicating my T-shirt with a flick of her chin. "You two take out your worries on your clothes."

I sigh and cross my arms. "I guess."

"Ay, niño, bad day?" Abuela asks, pulling Mom's scrubs top from her sewing machine and snipping a long thread with her scissors.

"Yeah. But whatever, it doesn't matter. I'll probably have to just start over somewhere else soon anyway after Dad gets posted in Alaska or something."

"Qué dramático. So pessimistic. It's not that bad, I'm sure." Abuela tries to reach for my hand, but I pull it away. She stands and grabs a small package from the stack of mail behind her. Handing it to me, she says, "Maybe this will make you feel better."

I take the package and turn it over in my hands. The all-caps writing makes my heart thud in my chest.

Dad.

His address is still the same: Bagram Air Base, Afghanistan. He hasn't moved.

I rip open the package and hold a book in my hands. It's dusty, and the cover is wrinkled. A smile starts to creep across my lips.

Dad and I started a tradition the last time he was deployed. We picked out a book, *The House on Mango Street*, mostly because Mom always went on and on about how it was her favorite book when she was growing up. Dad took it with him overseas and read it, making notes in the margins about things he liked. He wrote questions to me about what was happening. Then he mailed the book back so I could read it. I wrote answers to his questions and made my own observations. I even drew illustrations on some of the pages. Then I sent it back to him so he could read it again, see my answers and drawings, and answer my questions. We must've traded that book five times before he finally came home, each time writing in it more and more.

I flip through the pages of this book, *Sunrise over Fallujah* by Walter Dean Myers, and stop the first time I see Dad's handwriting. I press my fingers over his words, closing my eyes and imagining him sitting in his rack, reading. I flip through each page, looking for his handwriting, scanning for evidence of the life he lives when he's away from us. Dad says he has lots of time to read since the unofficial motto of the Army is "Hurry up and wait." There are long stretches of down-time, with short bursts of . . . activity.

I flip to another page and notice a smear on it. Is it coffee? Dirt?

Blood?

I snap the book shut and sigh. Even things that are supposed to bring Dad and me closer together make me worry more. Miss him more.

I drop the book in my lap.

Abuela clicks her tongue. "I thought that would make you feel better. Maybe not?"

I shake my head. All the book did was remind me of how far away Dad is, how I'm by myself. "You wouldn't understand. You don't know what it's like to have to start over. To have to be alone."

Abuela raises her eyebrows at me and pushes Mom's scrubs to the side. Her lips press into a hard line. She takes a deep breath.

"En serio, niño? I know nothing? I don't *understand*?" Her voice quivers, and her volume rises. I sit up straighter in my chair.

"My parents put me on a plane by myself when I was fourteen years old. Just two years older than you. I knew no one. I didn't speak English. I was leaving the only home, the only family, I had ever known. Don't you sit there and tell me I don't understand what it's like to start over."

My palms sweat, and I rub them on my jeans. "I'm sorry, Buela."

I should've known better than to make a comment like that to her. My bisabuelos sent Abuela to Florida all alone to escape Castro, the dictator of Cuba. She lived by herself for three years in Miami with two foster families she'd never even met before her parents were finally able to leave Cuba and join her.

Abuela gives me a sympathetic smile. She reaches

for my hand again, and this time, I let her take it. She runs her thumb over my knuckles. "Niño, I know this is difficult. But we'll make it through. We all will. You, me, your mami." She pauses and swallows. "Your papi."

I nod, looking at Abuela's hand. I notice three long scratches running the length of her forearm. The red angry lines match the jagged marks Talib and I saw on the tree in the woods.

Abuela's eyes dart to her arm, and she pulls the sleeve of her blouse down to her wrist. She pats my hand and says, "Todo va bien, niño. It'll all be okay."

She heads off to the kitchen, but I stay in my chair, pulling on the hem of my shirt until a long thread completely unravels from the fabric in a tangled web. I wrap the thread tightly around my finger over and over until it cuts off my circulation and turns the tip of my finger red. The sharp pain begs me to unwind the thread, but I don't, grateful for relief from the ache in my heart.

CHAPTER 9

I CLUTCH THE BOOK FROM DAD as I climb the stairs up to my room. Pushing the door open, I scan my room for the coyote.

He's sitting on my bed, staring out the window, a pile of half-chewed socks scattered around him.

"Hey," I say, picking up the socks. They're soaked with spit. "I helped you out. What's the deal?"

The coyote turns his head and blinks at me with his black eyes. "I got bored. Spent all day watching delicious rabbits and mice run through your backyard, and I had nothing to do."

"Well, thanks a lot." I grab my trash can and stuff the wet, holey socks into it. "You got a name?"

He scratches the blanket on my bed with his paw. "Rabbits call me brave. Squirrels call me mighty. Mice call me powerful."

"I call you liar," I mumble. The coyote doesn't hear me and rolls onto his back.

"You could call me any of those. Hey, what's the Spanish word for brave?"

"Valiente," I tell him. "But that's a lot. Maybe Val?"

"Works for me," Val says, licking his paw. "You know, I saw your grandma, too."

He hops down from my bed and trots gingerly over to me, not putting weight on his back leg.

"You're lucky she didn't see you. We would've had coyote roast for dinner." I set Dad's book on top of my dresser and place his compass next to it.

Val sits down on the carpet and licks his front paw. "Nah. She was in the woods all day."

"What?"

"In the woods. Not a smart choice, if you ask me." Val pauses his grooming and looks at me. "That's where the witch is."

The mystery in the woods is just the distraction I need from my horrible day.

"Okay, I need to know about this witch. I saved you from Brandon's trap. Now you get to return the favor."

Val huffs and rolls over to his back. "That's not very charitable of you. People should do good things without expecting anything in return."

"Sure. Thanks for the lesson. Now tell me about this witch."

He yawns, curling his tongue. "She's terrible. Just terrible. She chased me past the quarry. I didn't know wolverines could run so fast."

"So the witch is a wolverine?" I ask. That's an animal that would make anyone nervous in the woods. And it has no business being in Texas. Maybe Talib has good reason to be scared.

Scratching behind his ear with his uninjured back leg, Val says, "Yep. What I wouldn't give for opposable thumbs so I could throw rocks. One good smack on the nose and that witch wouldn't bother me anymore. Oh, and with thumbs, I could wring little bunnies' necks. That would be wonderful."

I shake my head and sit down on my bed. "Enough

with the thumbs. Tell me more about the witch. Why was she chasing you?"

Val pauses and thinks. "Well, other than I'm absolutely delicious, she probably wanted my power."

"Your power? What kind of power do you have?" I pull out my sketchbook and turn to a clean page.

Val narrows his eyes at me. "My fabulousness isn't immediately apparent to you?"

I roll my eyes. I write *witch* at the top of my sketchbook page and start drawing a wolverine underneath. I picture a long dark brown animal, bigger than a dog but smaller than a bear. Long, sharp claws erupt from its paws as knifepoint teeth jut from its lips. I shudder.

"If she bites me, she gets a coyote's power."

I shrug. "So she can kill small dogs and break into chicken coops."

Val snaps at my foot dangling from the bed. "No, so she can have super-sharp hearing, smell, and sight." He stares at me with beady black eyes. "I can see through your clothes right now."

I throw a pillow at him. "No, you can't."

I scrawl *wants other animals' powers* in my sketchbook before slamming it shut.

That night, I dream of a ferocious wolverine

prowling through the woods, snarling at Talib's lost dog as saliva drips from its fangs. The wolverine raises its arm, covered in matted brown fur, claws glistening in the moonlight as George cowers below, ready to be sliced to ribbons.

I wake up covered in sweat, my heart pounding in my ears.

It's still better than the dreams I usually have.

"Nestor! Niño!" I hear Abuela call from downstairs. "You have visitors!"

"Ya vengo!" I shout downstairs to let Abuela know I'm coming.

Val slept on my bed last night. We took turns kicking each other and tugging at the blankets. I know I need to get him out of my house. It's only a matter of time before Abuela goes into my room to get my laundry and her screams knock the entire house down.

I pull a duffel bag from the top shelf in my closet, and an old notebook drops to the floor. Flipping through the pages, I see sloppy drawings of animals with notes in the margins. The first page says, *Raúl Lopez's Animal Encyclopedia*. A smile creeps across my lips, but I shake my head. First things first.

Unzipping the duffel bag, I tell Val, "Look, you need to get out of here. Your leg is well enough, and my abuela will skin you alive if she finds you."

I dump the dart guns out of the bag and onto the floor of my closet and motion for him to jump in.

"That doesn't look very comfortable," he huffs, sniffing the edge of the bag.

"Neither is walking around without your fur. Jump in!" I hiss. "Hurry!"

Val settles into the bag, and I zip it shut. Gingerly lifting the straps onto my shoulder, I head downstairs.

Maria Carmen and Talib stand at the doorway. "Don't move," I whisper to Val as I head toward them.

"Hey, guys. What's up?"

Talib wrings his hands and doesn't answer. Finally, Maria Carmen says, "We need to practice our trivia questions more. I thought we could all go to Talib's house and go through our cards." She nudges Talib with her elbow, and he nods.

Maria Carmen and Talib have just given me the perfect excuse to get this coyote out of the house. "Sounds great!" I say a little too enthusiastically. I look at Abuela. "I'll be home before dinner. Te prometo."

"Okay, niño." She looks at the duffel bag hanging

off my shoulder and raises an eyebrow. My stomach flip-flops. "What's in the bag?" she asks.

My grip tightens around the strap of the bag. I pray the coyote won't move a muscle. "Just some dart guns I wanted to show Talib."

Abuela nods. "Bueno, have fun. Chao, pescao."

"Y a la vuelta, picadillo!" I respond, heading out the door and following Maria Carmen and Talib.

Talib looks at the duffel bag and says, "Dart guns? Awesome."

The coyote inside barks. Talib's eyes grow wide, and he jumps back.

"Yeah, not really. Just needed to get our injured friend out of the house." I look at Maria Carmen. "So how much studying are we going to do?"

A smile grows at the corner of Maria Carmen's mouth. "That wasn't exactly true, either. I had a different mission in mind." She points toward the woods behind our houses.

Talib groans. "The woods again? You said we really were going to study!"

Maria Carmen puts her hands on her hips. "Why would I drag you out of your house just to take you right back there?"

Talib bites his lip. "Oh yeah."

Val squirms in the bag. "So what's the real plan?" I ask. "I need to take this guy back anyway."

Maria Carmen pulls her backpack off her shoulders and unzips it. She reaches in and pulls out a pair of pliers. "I was thinking we could make sure that Brandon doesn't hurt any more animals in the woods. I know how we can dismantle all his traps. And we can look for Talib's dog. Maybe even my goats."

From inside the duffel bag, I hear a muffled, "Sounds good to me."

I chuckle. "I like the way you think. Let's go."

We head off into the woods. I find myself scanning behind every tree, bush, and cactus. Val's story about the witch has me a little spooked.

A lot like Talib was the first time we went through the woods.

Once we're deep enough in the trees, I lower my duffel bag to the ground and unzip it. Val crawls out and stretches, sticking his butt in the air. "You really couldn't have walked any slower, could you?"

"You're welcome," I tell him.

Maria Carmen laughs behind me. "Nestor, are you talking to that coyote?"

Talib shrugs. "He does that sometimes."

As much as I like Maria Carmen and Talib, I don't think I'm ready to tell them my big secret. I keep my mouth shut.

Val trots away from us, singing, "Here, bunny."

I stand and face Maria Carmen. "So let's find these traps."

Talib scuffs his feet on the ground. "You sure you don't actually have any dart guns in there, Nestor? You know, just in case we run into Brandon again." Talib pauses and looks around. "Or anything else."

Maybe keeping a couple of dart guns in the bag wouldn't have been a bad idea after all. Although, as effective as they would be against a snaggletoothed sixth grader, I'm not sure how much they'd do to keep a wolverine-witch away. Especially when we see a large century cactus smashed and torn to pieces on the ground, like a bulldozer had demolished it.

A foam dart definitely wouldn't stop whatever did that.

We spread out and start our search for Brandon's traps. Finally, after a few minutes, I hear Talib call, "Found one!"

Maria Carmen and I jog over to him. He's standing

over a rusty trap, just like the one we found clamped around Val's leg.

"Now what?" I ask.

Maria Carmen points the pliers at the small coils on each end of the trap. "If we take those out, the trap can't snap shut anymore. It'll just be a hunk of metal in the grass."

She crouches down, grabs a rock, and tosses it into the middle of the trap. The rock hits a small metal plate in the center, and the trap slams shut. Talib and I jump. Taking her pliers, Maria Carmen clamps them down on one coil and twists. She pulls the coil from the trap and tosses it to me. I drop it into my duffel bag. She does the same thing to the screw on the other side, and I deposit it with the other coil.

We make our way deeper into the woods, the winding branches of the live oak trees and thick mesquite bushes swallowing us in the hills. Our search turns up three more traps. One of them is covered in shed snakeskin. Talib tosses a rock onto each, and Maria Carmen makes quick work of the coils. I shake my duffel bag, the collection of metal coils growing.

"Are we sure all these traps are Brandon's?" Talib asks.

"Yeah. They're supposed to be tagged with the owner's name, phone number, and the date and time they were set. The fact that they don't have any of this pretty much guarantees they're Brandon's. He doesn't seem like he's much for rules," I tell him.

"You know a lot about this, Nestor," Maria Carmen says.

I shrug. "I was in Cub Scouts for a little bit in Kentucky."

"Just for a little bit?" she asks.

I hike the duffel bag higher up onto my shoulder, the coils rattling inside. "Well, there were always these father-son activities, and Dad was gone for most of them. Didn't really feel like doing it anymore."

Maria Carmen gives me a sympathetic smile and grabs my arm. "I . . . I need to tell you something."

I give her a questioning look. "What is it?"

"I heard my mom talking on the phone last night. She was telling someone she saw your abuela running through the woods a couple of nights ago. She was pretty upset about it."

My stomach starts to turn, and I grip the duffel bag tighter.

Maria Carmen sighs. "She thinks your abuela has

something to do with all the animals that are going missing."

My ears burn, and my pulse thuds in my fingers. "Do you?" I ask.

I don't want to tell her about the ear tags I found in Abuela's kitchen or her knife stuck in the mesquite bush in the woods.

Maria Carmen shakes her head. "No, I don't think so. But you need to know people are starting to talk."

Talib clears his throat next to us, his eyes scanning the hills. "Guys, I think that's probably enough for today, don't you?"

I look over a hill toward the quarry. The sun has started to set, stretching long shadows like snakes across the ground. Fallen air plants look like spiders creeping across the grass, their thin leaves sticking out in all directions. Thick tree trunks hide wolverines, their teeth ready to gnash at our throats.

"Yeah, I don't really want to be out here in the dark," Maria Carmen says, her voice shaking.

I slap Talib on the shoulder. "I completely agree."

CHAPTER 10

Hey, Dad!

We've got our first trivia competition in a few minutes, so this is going to be a quick letter.

So far things are okay in New Haven. I taught Maria Carmen and Talib to play dominoes. Abuelo would be proud. I didn't teach them all the words Abuelo used to say when we would play, though.

I found an old notebook of yours in my closet. It's an animal encyclopedia you made, complete with drawings and animal facts. Your drawings are . . . well, I'm glad you found a good job in the Army. Just kidding! Your notes are great. I can see who I get my animal-trivia knowledge from. But I think the animal facts you got from Abuela are hilarious. How does she know that armadillos love strawberries and that rabbits are terrified of migrating geese?

Don't tell Mom, but we went into the woods behind Abuela's house and got rid of some hunting traps that this jerk kid at school put there. It was the right thing to do, Dad, and you always taught me to do the right thing.

But still, please don't tell Mom.

Love you. Stay safe.
Nestor

I shut my sketchbook and slide it into my bag. This is one of the first letters I've written to Dad where I didn't have to lie to follow Mom's Always Be Positive, Always Be Happy rule.

Imagine that.

I head into the auditorium to get ready for our trivia competition. Miss Humala assures us she'll be proud no matter what. I know she's secretly hoping we get at least three answers right.

We're not off to the best start. Brandon trips Maria Carmen, sending her study cards flying across the auditorium stage, and when Talib bends down to help her pick them up, he smacks his head directly into her nose. Brandon snorts and pulls out my chair right as I sit down. My butt smacks hard onto the wood floor of the stage.

I don't think Brandon knows what we did to his traps yet. He's just being his usual, pleasant-as-an-exploding-skunk self.

Miss Humala sits in the front row of the audience, her head in her hands, muttering, "Three questions. Just three questions."

Abuela and Mom also sit in the front row, waving and smiling. Mom holds up her phone and snaps several pictures, giving me a salute.

A woman three rows behind them whispers to the man next to her and points to Abuela, a scowl pressed on her lips. I try not to think about what Maria Carmen told me.

Our opponents, four students from Burleson Middle School, march in and take their seats, frowns plastered to their faces. Either their teacher has threatened them with eternal detention scraping gum off desks, or the water in Burleson is tainted by a chemical that makes it impossible to smile.

Miss Humala gives us a half-hearted thumbs-up from her chair.

The moderator takes his place on the podium in front of us. He looks as though he has entered a contest for how far above his belly button he could wear his pants. And won.

Clearing his throat multiple times, Mr. Highpants eyes the microphone warily, probably checking to see if we were inspired by New Haven's previous trivia team and put glue on it. He taps the body of the microphone and, finding it glue-free, presses his mouth against it and breathes deeply. "All right, contestants. Let's begin. This competition will consist of ten toss-up questions worth 100 points each, which the team that buzzes in first will answer. If the answer is correct, the team will be asked a bonus question worth thirty points. Because this is our sixth-grade competition of the regional quiz bowl series, we will concentrate on the selected focus subject: zoology."

Maria Carmen smiles at Talib and me and twists a braid in her hand. She ignores Brandon. "We've got this, guys. I know we do."

"Contestants, please pick up your buzzers."

I try to focus on the incoming question, but all I can think about as I stare out at the audience is how much I want Dad here next to Mom and Abuela. He would love this.

Mr. Highpants breathes into the microphone, his voice sounding like a fast-food drive-through speaker. "What is a group of rhinoceros called?"

Just as I'm about to press my buzzer, Brandon smashes his next to me.

"What is a blob?" he says, looking at me and sneering. He knows that's not the right answer. He's trying to sabotage us.

Mr. Highpants shakes his head, and a blond pony-tailed girl from the Burleson team presses her buzzer. "A crash."

Maria Carmen stomps her foot under the table as Brandon snickers.

The Burleson team answers the bonus question correctly, and just like that, we're down 0–130.

I turn to Talib and whisper, "Whatever you do, buzz in before Brandon can. Even if you don't know the answer."

Mr. Highpants leans in closer to his mic. "With club-like appendages, what animal can strike so rapidly it creates vapor-filled bubbles underwater that shock prey and kill them?"

Talib smashes his buzzer over and over. "The mantis shrimp!"

We miss the bonus question because Brandon kicks Talib under the table when he tries to answer. 100–130.

Breathing heavily into the microphone, Mr. Highpants continues with the next question. "Which animal was incorrectly rumored to bury its head in the sand when frightened?"

A skeletal-looking boy from Burleson buzzes in. "Giraffe?"

The ponytailed girl elbows him so hard in the arm I'm afraid she's snapped it like a pretzel stick.

"I'm sorry, young man. That's incorrect." Mr. Highpants looks at our team.

I press my buzzer before Brandon can. "Ostrich."

"Well done, young man." Mr. Highpants smiles as

he hikes the waistband of his pants even farther up his chest.

We answer the bonus question right because Brandon is too distracted by the death stare Miss Humala is giving him. Three correct answers for our team. Miss Humala visibly relaxes in her seat. Mom and Abuela clap so much after each of our correct answers Mr. Highpants has to wait for them to stop before moving on to the next question.

The moderator fires more questions at us, and we trade correct answers with the Burleson team. Each time the Burleson team answers incorrectly, the ponytailed girl assaults the skeleton boy next to her with her elbow. He probably wishes he'd gone out for the football team instead. That way he could have been obliterated in one tackle, instead of little by little by an overenthusiastic teammate.

By the last question, I look at the score tally and see we're down by only one round, 430–530. If we get the last answer correct, we tie. And if we get the bonus question, we win. Miss Humala perches on the edge of her chair, her long red nails digging into the armrest. Mom holds her phone up, videoing the whole thing. Maria Carmen bounces up and down in her seat and takes a deep breath. "We've got this. We've got this. I know we've got this."

Brandon leans toward me and whispers, "Get ready to lose."

Mr. Highpants clears his throat loudly into the microphone. "With the ability to revert back to its juvenile polyp stage, this animal can repeatedly delay death."

Brandon smashes his buzzer, but the ponytailed girl rings in first. Mr. Highpants points at her, and she leans forward, announcing in her microphone, "Man-of-war."

Mr. Highpants wipes sweat off his sun-starved forehead as we eagerly await his judgment. He gives a long sigh. "I'm sorry, that's incorrect."

I slam my elbow into Brandon's side as Talib presses his buzzer furiously. "Immortal jellyfish!" he cries out before Mr. Highpants even acknowledges him. The ponytailed girl slams her fist on the table and glares daggers at us.

Mr. Highpants gives us a wry smile. "That is correct. We are tied." He takes his time pulling out the card with our bonus question.

"All right, contestants. Final question." He yanks on

the waistband of his pants. "This animal's name also means 'glutton,' due to its ferocious appetite and habit of eating quickly, leaving nothing behind after slashing its prey with its sharp claws and teeth."

A boulder drops in my stomach. I swallow hard. Maria Carmen flips a braid in Brandon's face and distracts him. I press my buzzer, and Mr. Highpants looks at me, licking his lips. "A . . . a wolverine," I stammer.

"Correct! New Haven wins!" Mr. Highpants claps. Maria Carmen lets out a yelp next to me, and Talib jumps in his chair. Brandon smacks his forehead on the table. I ignore them, my heart still beating in my ears. Miss Humala jumps up onto the stage and wraps her arms around me. She pulls me into a hug, thankfully quick, since there's nothing worse than being hugged by a teacher. She moves on to the rest of our team, but instead of hugging Brandon, she places a firm hand on his shoulder and presses her lips together.

"Not a good start, Brandon. Not a good start," she says, shaking her head.

Brandon shrugs off her hand and stomps out of the auditorium.

Abuela and Mom run up to me onstage, smiling and clapping.

"Victory selfie!" Mom cries, holding her phone out. Talib, Maria Carmen, and I crowd around her as she snaps a picture. She manages to cut out half of Talib's face and both of Maria Carmen's eyes. Still, I'm glad Dad will get to see my new friends.

Even if it's just parts of them.

Abuela wraps me in a lavender-scented hug. "Felicidades, mi niño!"

"Thanks, Buela," I tell her.

Looking out into the seats in the auditorium, I notice the woman who had been whispering behind Abuela is now talking to three more people. They're all looking at us with narrow eyes and tight lips.

I want to know what they're saying, but I'm afraid to find out.

Returning to Talib, I give him a high five. He's still grinning and bouncing on his toes. Talib breathes a sigh of relief. "Didn't think we'd have to play against our own teammate." I look past him and see Miss Humala hurry to the side of the stage, behind a curtain.

"This is ridiculous," Maria Carmen says, hands on

hips. "Can't Brandon clean up trash in the cafeteria or something? Why does he have to be on our team?"

I think that's an excellent question for Miss Humala, but she seems busy talking to someone offstage. I can't make out what she's saying, but she's waving her hands around wildly, and her cheeks are flushed. She looks angry.

I step away from Maria Carmen and Talib to see if I can tell who Miss Humala is arguing with. As I draw closer, an enormous brown snake slithers away from her . . . and out the back doors behind the stage.

CHAPTER 11

WHEN YOU GO TO AS MANY SCHOOLS as I have, you meet a lot of teachers. Some bother to learn your name; some don't. Some don't realize they're sticking their butt in your face every time they lean down to help the clueless kid sitting next to you. Some let out a maniacal cackle every time you get a multiplication fact wrong. At Fort Lewis in Washington, I had a PE teacher who would give you extra credit if you could stuff more marshmallows into your mouth than he could (ten bonus points for me!). But I've never had a teacher who argued with a ten-foot scaly snake.

Between this and the wolverine-witch roaming the woods, New Haven has more weird than I want to handle.

I shake my head, trying to fling the image of the huge brown snake from my brain, and focus on our win. Maria Carmen, Talib, and I burst out of the side doors of the auditorium.

Trouncing the Burleson team feels good—especially considering how sour their faces were and how hard Brandon worked against us.

"I knew we could do it, guys." Maria Carmen claps, grinning.

"Yeah, it was pretty cool." I put my hand up, and Maria Carmen and I high-five. We did better than I thought we would, and what's more, I didn't have to move again before our first competition. That must be some kind of record. If I'm in New Haven long enough, we might even have a shot at the championship.

If only I could be here in May.

Talib slaps me on the back. "Hey, I've got an idea. Let's go down to the pharmacy to celebrate."

"The pharmacy? How are we planning to celebrate?"

I ask. "Covering ourselves in superhero Band-Aids? Checking who has the highest blood pressure?"

Talib laughs and shakes his head. "They sell ice cream there."

"I've got a better idea," Maria Carmen chimes in. "Let's go to my house. My mom promised to make churros if we won. I just texted her the good news."

I'd pick fried dough drenched in cinnamon and sugar over questionable pharmacy ice cream any day. We head to Maria Carmen's house, which takes about two seconds since New Haven is small enough to be undetectable on any map. I think it's covered by the *x* in *Texas*.

And we decide not to go through the woods.

Maria Carmen lives just beyond where Talib and I do, a little outside of town. Her house sits on a large piece of land covered with live oak and cedar trees. I notice a broken wooden fence at the corner of her yard, splintered and scattered on the ground. That must've been how her goats got out.

Or how something got in.

As we skip up the gravel driveway to Maria Carmen's house, still riding high from our victory, a tall, slender woman bursts from the front door. "Felici-dades!" she cries, raising her arms in the air.

"Thank you, Mami," Maria Carmen says, kissing her mom on the cheek.

Maria Carmen's mom ushers us into their house. "Talib, mijo, how are you?"

"Good, Ms. Cordova. Thanks." Talib shuffles behind Maria Carmen into the kitchen.

Ms. Cordova looks at me with a smile. "And you are?"

"Nestor Lopez. Nice to meet you," I tell her.

The smile disappears from Ms. Cordova's lips. Her eyes narrow and look me up and down. "Guadalupe Lopez's grandson?"

"Yes, ma'am."

Without a word, Ms. Cordova turns on her heel and heads into the kitchen, leaving me alone. I bite my lip, remembering the phone call Maria Carmen told me about. Her mom still seems angry.

I head into the kitchen and sit next to Maria Carmen at the table. Ms. Cordova sets plates in front of us, and I pretend to ignore that she slams my plate down a little harder than the others, even though it makes me jump.

Maria Carmen takes churros from the basket in front of us and piles them on each of our plates.

"These look amazing, Ms. Cordova," Talib says, licking his lips.

I have to admit, the fresh churros smell delicious.

"Gracias, mijo," Ms. Cordova replies, using a slotted spoon to lift more churros out of a large pot of boiling oil on the stove. She places them on a paper towel, which soaks up the excess oil, then drops them into a bowl filled with cinnamon and sugar. The sugar glistens in the low light of the kitchen.

"Anything for my conquering heroes," she adds, patting Talib on the back. She takes another churro from the basket and tosses it on the mountain Talib already has on his plate.

Talib swallows the last bite of his churro and adds two more to his plate. "Do you still need me to help fix your fence this weekend?"

Ms. Cordova turns toward us from the stove. "That would be wonderful." She lowers her eyes at me. "Nestor should come, too. It's the least he can do."

"Mami, deja," Maria Carmen says, shushing her mom.

Ms. Cordova slams her spoon down on the kitchen

counter, oil splattering on her hand, and storms into the living room.

"Geez, Nestor. You make a really good first impression," Talib says.

"It's not his fault. Mami still thinks his abuela had something to do with our goats," Maria Carmen replies.

Talib stares at me. "Really? Do *you* think she did, Nestor?"

I wipe cinnamon and sugar from my hands on my jeans. "Of course not."

The image of Abuela stomping off between the trees flashes in my mind. The long scratches on her arm. The coyote's telling me about her spending the day in the woods. "Of course not," I say again, trying to convince myself just as much as Maria Carmen and Talib.

Talib grabs another churro and shoves it into his mouth. "I know she didn't. It was probably that wolverine-snake thing that took my dog."

Maria Carmen nods. "I know you saw it, too."

I shake my head. "Wait. What are you guys talking about?"

Maria Carmen brushes the cinnamon and sugar from her hands. "I know it wasn't your abuela. The night our goats went missing, I saw a huge brown snake slithering through our backyard. Mami didn't believe me. She said shock was making me see things."

She slides the basket of churros over to Talib, who takes two more. "I thought she was right. Maybe I was just seeing things. It wasn't until I told Talib what I saw that he told me about his dog."

Swallowing a mouthful of churro, Talib says, "Poor George. It's one thing to get attacked by a wolverine. Another thing to get dragged off by a snake. But both?" Talib shakes his head. "I saw that wolverine in the woods when I was trying to find George. Then its fur started flying off it, and it changed into a snake. A huge brown one. I thought maybe I had eaten a bad breakfast taco."

"I still can't believe you named your dog George," I say.

"Focus, Nestor," Maria Carmen says. "We all know there's something in the woods. Something weird that shouldn't be there. A wolverine or a snake. Or both."

I push my plate away, the sweet churros rolling around in my stomach. "We have to do something about it. I can't let anyone think my abuela has anything to do with this. I know people were talking about her at our competition."

Maria Carmen looks down, pressing her fingers to the sugar on her plate. "I'm sorry, Nestor. We'll figure this out."

We make a plan to meet at Talib's house tomorrow and search the woods for the witch. I'm not sure what we'll do if we find her.

Probably run and scream. That seems like a totally normal reaction to facing a wolverine-snake witch.

My stomach full of fried dough and sugar, I look out the kitchen window at the setting sun. I need to get back home soon, so I make my way through Maria Carmen's living room and stop in my tracks when I look above her fireplace. Perched on the mantel is a US flag, wrapped in the shape of a triangle, only the blue field with white stars showing. The flag is set in a glass-front triangular box.

It's the flag given to soldiers' families when they're buried.

The flag they draped over the coffin of Maria Carmen's brother.

A hard lump rises in my throat, and my stomach churns.

Maria Carmen stands next to me, and her eyes follow mine to the mantel. She goes over and pulls down a framed picture next to the flag. She runs her fingers along the glass, over the face of a man in his dress uniform, a shiny silver iron cross with two circles hanging off his jacket. I recognize it as a sharpshooter medal. Dad has the same one.

"He looks brave, doesn't he?" she asks me, tears glistening in the corners of her eyes.

I swallow hard. "He does. He really does."

Maria Carmen returns the picture to the mantel and wipes her eyes. She looks at me with a weak smile. "I'm glad you're here. After Carlos died, all my friends were really nice at first. But then they got upset that I was still sad. Talib was the only one who stuck around."

I smile. That doesn't surprise me. Talib seems like the kind of friend who won't forget to write you.

Maria Carmen sighs. "You know, Nestor, just because it happened to my brother . . . doesn't mean your dad—"

I inhale a sharp breath.

"I know," I say. "Thanks. I've got to go."

I burst from the front door, chased by images of

soldiers rolling down dusty streets in Humvees, never knowing what's around the next corner, down the next street.

The concrete hurts my feet as I run down the sidewalk. I make a sharp left and cut between two houses, into the woods. The sun has almost completely set, and the sky is a fiery red. My lungs burn as I trip over tree roots and rocks. I don't care what's in the woods, whether a wolverine is going to rip my throat out or a snake is going to squeeze me until my eyeballs pop. It's nothing compared with what Dad is facing thousands of miles away.

A green blur slams into me and knocks me to the ground. I struggle against it, but my arms are pinned down.

"You destroyed my traps," Brandon says, his hot breath hissing in my face.

"Of course I did." I squirm underneath him, but he presses me down, rocks cutting into my back.

"You can't do that." Brandon releases my arm and slams his fist into the ground next to my head.

I kick my leg out and roll from under him. Jumping to my feet, I shout, "You can't tell me what to do. And you can't hunt whatever you feel like."

"No, no. You don't understand." Brandon crouches in the dirt and pounds his fists into the ground, the rocks scraping his knuckles. "She needs them."

I brush my hands on my jeans. "What are you talking about?"

Brandon looks at me and wipes the back of his hand across his face. His bloody knuckles leave a streak of red across his mouth.

"The witch. She made me set them."

CHAPTER 12

"YOU'VE SEEN THE WITCH?" I ask Brandon.

He launches himself up from the ground and rushes at me. I drop to the grass and roll to my side, missing Brandon's tackle. He slams into a tree with a grunt.

Panting, he sits against the tree trunk, struggling to catch his breath. "You know, a lot of people in town say you're living with the witch."

"My abuela is *not* the witch."

I kick a rock, and it hits Brandon in the thigh. He grabs it, tossing it up and down in his hand. His chest heaves, and he starts to laugh. The unnerving sound spreads through the evening air.

"They don't know about the real witch. But they sure think your grandma has something to do with all the missing animals," he sneers. "It'd be bad if someone told them she was up to worse."

I kick another rock and stomp toward Brandon. "You don't get to say anything about my abuela. Leave her alone."

Brandon jumps up and shoves me hard in the chest. The air pushes from my lungs, and I choke. "Then leave my traps alone. She's gonna be mad at me. So, so mad."

I stand my ground. "I'm not letting you . . . or her . . . hurt anyone else."

"Oh yeah?" Brandon grabs my T-shirt with one hand and raises his fist, aimed right for my nose.

I squeeze my eyes shut, waiting for the blow that will rearrange the angle of my face.

Instead, I hear, "Aw, man! Gross!"

I open my eyes and see a thick, milky glob dripping down Brandon's cheek. He lets go of my shirt and wipes it away with his hand.

"Is this . . . ?"

"White lightning!" squawks Cuervito above me.

"That's nasty!" Brandon cries as a squirrel jumps down from the tree onto his head. It pulls his hair and scratches his ears as he waves his arms around wildly. Brandon grabs the squirrel and throws it to the ground. It scampers up the tree and says to me, "We got you, buddy. Don't worry."

Brandon looks at me, cheeks red, chest heaving.

"Fire in the hole!" I hear above me. I take a step back in case Cuervito's aim isn't very good.

Brandon shoves me aside and takes off through the trees, the squirrel scampering behind him and Cuervito soaring above. His shouts disappear into the sky.

I lean back against an oak tree to catch my breath.

A bully chased off by a lunatic squirrel and a daredevil raven.

A witch that may be a wolverine. Or a snake.

As I jog toward Abuela's house, I rehearse in my head how exactly I'm going to explain New Haven to Dad.

Turns out my chance comes sooner than I expected.

I hear a call from upstairs the moment I enter Abuela's house.

"Nestor! Hurry! Come up here!" Mom shouts.

I bound up the stairs two at a time and find Mom sitting on her bed with her laptop in front of her.

"What is it?" I ask, breathless.

"Your dad wants to talk to you," she says, her smile stretching ear to ear. Her hand clutches Dad's ring on her necklace as she motions me to the bed.

Mom hands me the laptop and kisses the top of my head. "Have a good talk," she says, heading downstairs.

"Thanks, Mom," I call after her. I look at the small square on the screen holding Dad's video chat. It's surrounded by the background on Mom's computer—a collage of pictures I've drawn. I smile as I look over sharks, eagles, tigers, even Chela the deer. Mom has kept all my drawings, in her own way.

Dad waves at me from the screen. I wonder how I'm going to spin "there's an evil witch in the woods, and I think Abuela might know something about it" to fit Mom's Always Be Positive, Always Be Happy requirement.

I've got nothing.

"Hey, buddy. How's school? Find anything good in town?" Dad asks. His ACUs (advanced combat uniform) look like they've been repeatedly washed in dust. His normally close-cut hair is a little longer than the last time we video chatted, and I can spot flecks of gray in it. His chin has a new scar that tells a story I'll probably never hear.

"Oh, it's good. It's all good. Nothing special," I offer with a lackluster smile. A witch forced the school bully to set traps in the woods, and Abuela's covering up scratches from whatever she's doing in secret. Yep, totally normal.

"Well, buddy, you know I appreciate your taking care of your mom." He runs his hand through his hair. I notice cuts on his knuckles and wonder how they got there. "I know it's hard, but you do a good job of being man of the house."

I don't bother to tell Dad that I managed to sweeten Abuela's café con leche this morning with salt instead of sugar or that the breakfast taco I destroyed in the microwave is now a permanent fixture on the kitchen ceiling.

Before Dad's first deployment, he took me to the bowling alley at Fort Carson, Colorado. We gorged ourselves on cheap nachos and Coke as Dad pointed out which of his commanding officers had a worse bowling score than he did (all of them). He told me random military trivia, like how they tried to train bats to drop bombs during World War II. Between gutter balls and strikes, he told me I was the man of the house and needed to look after my mom.

I was in second grade.

"I got the drawing you sent." Dad holds up a picture of a reddish-brown coyote jumping up in the air to snatch the black raven flying above him. "This one's really good." I don't tell him that one was drawn from real life as Val jumped up and down on my bed.

"Hey, I got one for you. You're never going to get this one." Dad smirks and rubs his hands together.

I know what's coming.

Dad clears his throat and folds his hands in front of him, doing his best impression of a game show host. "What animal lets out a bloodcurdling, laugh-like cry after it makes a successful kill?"

Please don't let it be a wolverine. I think for a moment and smack a pillow on Mom's bed. Dad's image shakes on the computer screen. "Easy. Hyena!"

Dad laughs. "I thought I had you for sure."

"Have you seen any hyenas over there?"

"Nah, we've been . . . busy." Dad looks down, and

there's an awkward pause in our conversation. Then his head pops up. "Made friends?"

He always asks me this. I think he forgets that the instant camaraderie in the military doesn't exactly happen in middle school. It's a little more like cage-match fights to the death with cafeteria burritos and chocolate pudding.

Instead, I offer, "Yeah, there's one kid who's pretty cool. He's sure his dog got eaten by a wolverine. My other friend had her goats taken by a huge snake. And there's a bully who's working with a witch."

Dad pinches his eyebrows together. "What'd you say, buddy? I think the connection glitched."

I pick at the hem of my shirt. "Nothing."

We finish our video chat with our usual "Love you, stay safe." I stare at the blank screen long after Dad has clicked off. Replaying our conversation in my head, I remember his voice, the way he scrunches his sunburned nose up when he laughs. I wish I could've reached into the computer and pulled him right through. That way, he'd be safe, and I'd have someone to help me make sense of this crazy town.

I close the laptop and head into my room. Taking Dad's compass out of my pocket, I set it next to my sketchbook. I'm about to flip to my Days in New Haven page when a dull thud against my bedroom window distracts me. I look at the large sycamore tree outside the window and see one of the thick branches pushing against the glass.

Except it's not a branch. It's a snake.

Her tail is wrapped around a branch pointed toward the house, and she's stretching her body out to the window. She smacks her brown snout against the glass. I shoot my eyes toward the window latch to see if it's sealed.

It's not.

The snake gives one more hard thud against the window and pushes it open, launching herself into my room and onto the floor.

"Well, that was a little more work than I care to do," she hisses, curling her body and raising her head. "You should come to me next time, no? I've seen you meandering through the woods enough, my dear."

I step back from the snake. "Excuse me?"

"Yes, you've spent plenty of time in the woods. Making a mess of things," the snake responds, inching closer to me.

I'm pretty certain this is the same snake Maria

Carmen saw in her backyard. That took all her goats. And did something to Talib's dog in the woods. My throat closes up when I try to suck in a breath.

I choose my words carefully. "So, um, if you don't mind my asking, what exactly are you doing in the woods in Texas?"

Where a snake like you has absolutely no business?

I try again to step away from the snake, but she slithers closer, closing the gap between us.

"You get right to the point, don't you?" the snake says, flicking her black tongue in and out. "I'm surprised your grandmother hasn't filled you in. I'm simply here to take in some sun."

I look around my room, wondering if I can lunge for the dart guns dumped on the floor of my closet before this snake can give me a suffocating hug. Not that a foam dart would do much damage against something that could coil around me and snap my spine like uncooked spaghetti.

"You need to keep your grandmother out of the woods," the snake says, her black beady eyes fixed on me. "You and your friends would do good to steer clear as well. You've already done enough damage."

My heart is thudding in my stomach, and I'm

desperate to get this snake out of my room. But I'm so tired of not knowing what's going on. Not knowing what Abuela is doing in the woods. Not knowing what exactly this witch is up to. Not knowing everything that's going on with Dad. I swallow hard and say, "Why did I see you talking to Miss Humala?"

The snake tilts her head and flicks her tongue out. She begins to slither toward the window, and I try to contain my growing relief.

"Oh, my dear, you can't expect me to tell you everything. How silly."

The snake reaches the window and turns toward me. "Just stay out of my way, let me do what I came to do, and you'll be fine. If you choose to continue your little adventures through the woods and into my business . . . well, I can practically feel what it would be like to squeeze the last breath out of you."

I swallow hard. "So . . . so you're the witch?" I stammer.

The snake pauses. Her tongue flicks the window-pane. "A witch? Oh, I'm something so much better."

She extends her body out the window and reaches the branch of the sycamore tree. Curling her body around the branch, she begins to slither down the tree.

Turning to flick her tongue at me one last time, she says, "Don't disappoint me."

My stomach churns as I watch the snake slither through Abuela's backyard and into the woods.

I go downstairs and ask Abuela if she has a hammer so I can nail my window shut.

CHAPTER 13

I'M GETTING ANSWERS TODAY. No matter what.

Dad calls this forward observation. When they come across a bomb that's been hidden in a building or buried on the side of the road, they send in a remote-controlled robot to investigate the area. I got to drive one at a family day at Fort Carson. It had a camera on the end that let you see exactly where a threat was.

Unfortunately, I don't have an EOD robot to run around the woods behind Abuela's house. Dad and I started to build one with parts we'd ordered little by little, but the unfinished pieces are scattered among a handful of boxes in my closet. I'm going to have to stomp around out there, not knowing if a giant snake is curled up in a cedar tree, ready to give me a death hug. Or if a wolverine is hiding behind a mesquite bush, waiting to sharpen its claws on my stomach.

I plan to round up Talib and Maria Carmen. Safety in numbers.

But first, breakfast.

I head downstairs and pause at the bottom step. I can hear Mom talking to Abuela in the kitchen, her voice tight. It makes me nervous.

And think of Dad.

"Lupe, what's going on?" I hear my mom say. "Some random woman came up to me in the grocery store yesterday, ranting about how you needed to stay away from her chickens. She said she saw you running around between her yard and the woods. I had no idea what she was talking about."

"No es nada, mi amor. Just talk. Nothing to worry about," Abuela replies.

"Well, she practically rammed me with her shopping cart. Not sure why she would be so mad about nothing."

I round the corner, clearing my throat as I enter the kitchen. "Morning, Buela. Morning, Mom."

Abuela and Mom stop their conversation and smile at me, Mom's lips a tight line across her face.

I walk over to the stove, where Abuela is frying ham croquetas, the breakfast of champions. I pick one up and start to pop it in my mouth.

"Dejalos en paz. They're still hot," Abuela says beside me. Her yellow daisy housecoat swishes back and forth to the sound of Celia Cruz's "Quimbara" playing from the small radio in the corner of the kitchen.

I put down the freshly fried croqueta, the crunchy bread crumb coating sticking to my fingers. I can practically taste the salty ham filling, making me forget about my scaly visitor last night. At least for a few seconds.

The doorbell rings, and Mom rises slowly from the kitchen table, still tired from her overnight shift at the hospital.

"How much longer?" I ask, my mouth already watering.

Abuela clicks her tongue. "Ay, sin paciencia."

We hear a thud come from the living room, followed by Mom's shouting, "No! No!"

I look at Abuela. She drops her wooden spoon, and we race out of the kitchen. Mom is crouched on the floor, hugging her knees, muttering no over and over.

At the front door stand two men in uniform. My heart jumps into my throat, and I run over to Mom. I wrap my arms around her, squeezing her as she shakes.

This can't be happening. My brain flashes to the flag folded on Maria Carmen's mantel. Mom always hated answering the door wherever we lived, afraid it would be men in uniform notifying us that the worst had happened to Dad.

Looking again at the uniformed men, I squeeze my eyes closed and then open again. They aren't men. They're kids. High schoolers, to be exact, probably from the ROTC program.

One of them clears his throat and extends a flyer to us. "Um, would you like to buy some popcorn?"

Abuela gives them a sympathetic smile. "Sorry, niños. We're fine. No popcorn today, I think."

"Okay, thank you, ma'am," one of the boys says. They shuffle down our front walk, casting one last glance at Mom, who's still in my arms on the floor.

I brush the hair from her face and whisper in her ear. "It's not what you thought. It's okay. Dad's okay."

Mom takes a deep breath, her head still sagging. "I know. I know it's stupid. It's just that when I first saw them . . ."

I grab her hands and squeeze. "You thought they were coming to tell you something happened to Dad."

Mom lifts her head and looks at me. "I didn't really see them. All I saw was their uniforms. It's silly, but I've thought about that . . ." Her voice catches in her throat, and she presses her hand over her mouth.

I press my forehead to Mom's. Taking a deep breath, I struggle to keep my voice from quivering. "I know. I have, too."

Abuela puts her arms around Mom, and we help her stand up. Wiping the tears from her cheeks, Mom gives a weak laugh. "Those poor boys must think I'm insane."

I look at Mom and notice the deep wrinkles that climb from the corners of her eyes to her temples. I shrug. "I don't think so. They probably just think you really hate popcorn."

"Niño," Abuela chides me, playfully smacking me on the back of the head.

"I think I'm going to lie down for a bit," Mom says, her cheeks still flushed.

I help her up the stairs, her weight leaning on me more with each step. She's always been the strong one, the one rubbing my back when I cry about Dad's missing something at school or home, when I worry about what I've seen on the news. Holding her up as she weakens with each stair, I feel a weight I'm not used to carrying.

As I tuck her under the covers of her bed, I kiss her on the cheek. "He'll be okay, Mom."

She doesn't answer and rolls away from me. Her long sigh fills the room as she deflates under the blanket.

I put my hand on her shoulder and give it a light squeeze.

"People forget the middle," I say quietly, knowing my mom is barely listening. "There are always parades when he leaves and parties when he comes back. But nobody talks about the middle."

Pulling the comforter up over her shoulder, I sigh. "Nobody talks about this."

I trudge down the stairs, back into the kitchen.

Abuela sits at the table, a café con leche in her hand. "How is she?" Abuela asks.

I open my mouth to answer, but the words are blocked in my throat by years of Dad's absence. Missed school plays, science fairs, family dinners, Christmases, and birthdays. But there's always the hope that he'll be here for the next one. Yes, don't worry, he'll be here next time.

Today reminds me that there's always a chance there won't be a next time.

And this thought makes my shoulders sink as I blink back tears.

Abuela holds out her arms, and I let her wrap me in a field of daisies, my sobs flooding their petals.

CHAPTER 14

I MAY NOT BE ABLE TO DO ANYTHING for Dad, so far away. But I can help Abuela. I can make the people in town understand that she doesn't have anything to do with the disappearing animals. And I can keep the witch from doing any more damage.

I texted Talib and Maria Carmen, telling them we needed to put our woods search on hold until Monday. Mom, Abuela, and I spent the weekend co-cooned in blankets on the couch, bingeing telenovelas and leftover ham croquetas as I flipped through Dad's animal encyclopedia. Abuela and Mom argued over whether we should watch *Amor Peligroso*, *Amor Baboso*, or *Amor Amoroso de los Amores*. I just buried my head in Abuela's shoulder and inhaled her lavender perfume.

At least Abuela didn't go into the woods. Hopefully that's enough for the snake to leave us alone.

I take the route through town to get to school instead of walking through the woods. Running into a murderous snake or wolverine would probably make me late for class.

Maria Carmen, Talib, and I huddle together in the back of the auditorium, waiting for Principal Jelani to calm down the hurricane of students so his assembly on "Understanding Your Changing Body" can begin.

"So what's our pick today?" Maria Carmen asks, holding a stack of trivia cards in her hand. "Prepare for our upcoming competition or research the evil witch terrorizing the town?"

Talib slouches in his seat. "Decisions, decisions."

"Witch. Definitely witch," I say a little too quickly. Maria Carmen and Talib look at me. I don't want to tell them about my scaly nighttime visitor. There's no way I can say what went on without revealing my big secret. "I, uh, think fighting off impending doom beats winning a Texas regional quiz competition."

"But think of the honor. The glory!" Talib jokes.

"Think of not getting ripped to shreds by a wolverine," Maria Carmen retorts.

"Oh, yeah. That. So where do we start?"

Nervous, I drum my fingers on my armrest. "I actually have a couple of clues."

Maria Carmen shoves the trivia cards into her backpack. "What?"

Swallowing hard, I take a deep breath. "After our competition the other day, I saw Miss Humala talking to a huge snake backstage in the auditorium. I think she might have something to do with the wolverine-snake witch."

Talib's mouth drops open. "She was talking to a snake? Just like a person?"

"Yeah, it happens, I guess," I say, rubbing the back of my neck. I don't want to tell them I could hear the snake say, "Don't stop me," as she slithered out of the auditorium. "And then there's Brandon."

"What? He's actually the witch? That would make sense," Talib says, scanning the auditorium for signs of our favorite camo-wearing sixth grader.

"No. After I left your house"—I point to Maria Carmen—"I ran into Brandon in the woods. Or, rather, he ran into me. Hard. He said the witch was making him set the traps."

Maria Carmen chews her bottom lip. "So when we dismantled Brandon's traps . . ."

"There's a chance we ticked off a psychotic witch who can slash our throats as a wolverine and wring us out like a meat towel as a snake."

Talib puts his head in his hands. "Fantastic."

"So where do we go from here?" Maria Carmen asks.

"I think we should go to Miss Humala's classroom and do some investigating," I tell them. I don't tell them that I actually plan to interrogate Milla, the class chinchilla.

Baby steps.

"Okay, but I'm not sure what you think you'll find," Maria Carmen says.

Talib keeps an eye out, checking for when Miss Humala abandons her post at the side of the auditorium. He nudges me and points toward the back door. Miss Humala clicks down the aisle in her high heels, her lips pressed together, eyes narrowed into slits.

She looks like she's about to skin a baby seal and eat it for lunch. We see her put a firm hand on Brandon's shoulder to hiss something into his ear.

The three of us sneak out of the auditorium and make our way to Miss Humala's classroom. We scan the room filled with cat skeletons and jars of frogs preserved in formaldehyde. Maria Carmen makes her way to Miss Humala's desk. Talib follows her.

I head straight to Milla's cage. She's sitting on her hind legs, scratching her belly. I tap my finger on the metal bars. "Hey, Milla."

Milla stares at me with large black eyes. "You bring me mango slices? Carrot sticks? The kid in charge of feeding me keeps forgetting. Stupid Job of the Week list."

"No, sorry, buddy," I whisper. I hope Maria Carmen and Talib are too busy searching Miss Humala's desk to notice I'm chatting up the class pet.

Milla shakes her head and scratches her long gray tail. "Fine. Guess I'll just waste away to nothing. Hopefully there's a 'dispose of dead chinchilla' on the Job of the Week list."

"Hey, I got a question for you," I tell Milla, pretending to look at the books on the shelf behind her cage. "Does Miss Humala ever have any visitors in here?"

Milla pauses. "Visitors? Why would you want to know about visitors?" She scurries up to the ledge in her cage and buries herself in the fabric hammock strung between two bars.

I move to the cabinets next to the bookcase and whisper, "Any chance you've seen her talking to a snake?"

"Find anything over there, Nestor?" I hear Maria Carmen ask behind me.

I open a cabinet, and a waterfall of animal pelts tumbles out. I shriek and jump back, knocking over an empty beaker. I catch it just before it rolls to the floor.

"Just a mild heart attack," I say. "Keep looking over there."

Maria Carmen and Talib keep rifling through the drawers in Miss Humala's desk.

Milla peeks out at me. "You know the snake?"

"We may have been introduced a few nights ago," I whisper.

Milla's small hands clutch the fabric hammock. "Be careful. Oh, you must be careful. I've seen her talk to the snake, too. Two months ago, it crawled through the

162

window and had a huge argument with Miss Humala. Thought I was going to be a prelunch snack for sure."

"Really?" I think back to what Maria Carmen and Talib told me about Miss Humala's switch from peppermint-sharing teacher to scowling dictator. It must have happened about the same time.

"Yes, that snake is vicious. Stay away from it. Stay out of the woods, whatever you do!"

"Nestor, the assembly is almost over," Maria Carmen says behind me. "We've got to go."

"Okay," I tell them. "Did you guys find anything?"

"Only that Miss Humala really loves beef jerky," Talib says. "There's a mountain of wrappers in her desk."

"They're really old, too," Maria Carmen says. She lifts a wrapper up to show me. "Some of them are covered in cobwebs. Nasty."

"That's from the snake," Milla says next to me.

"What? What does that have to do with the snake?" I whisper to Milla.

"She's not just a snake," Milla squeaks.

Talib closes the drawers in Miss Humala's desk and says, "Nestor, quit talking to that chinchilla and let's go."

If he only knew.

Maria Carmen and Talib straighten the things on Miss Humala's desk as I put back everything that fell out of the cabinets. I'm shoving the last of the animal pelts onto their shelf when I hear, "What exactly are you doing in my classroom?"

CHAPTER 15

"**WHY AREN'T YOU AT THE ASSEMBLY?**" Miss Humala's eyes dart around the classroom. I hope we put everything back in its place.

Maria Carmen steps forward and stammers, "We . . . we were looking for more animal-trivia cards to study."

"Why would you skip an assembly to get trivia cards?" Miss Humala narrows her eyes at us. I can hear Talib swallow hard next to me.

I clear my throat. "It was my fault, Miss Humala.

I made them come with me. I don't like school assemblies."

Miss Humala puts her hands on her hips. "Why on earth not?"

Scuffing my feet on the floor, I shove my hands into my pockets. "During my dad's second deployment, I started watching all these videos of surprise military reunions on YouTube. You know the ones? The dad surprising his family at a football game, the mom sneaking up on her kids in the middle of the cafeteria. My mom made me quit watching them because every day I'd come home from school upset my dad hadn't surprised me that day."

"Really?" Talib asks next to me.

Maria Carmen gives him a hard stare, and he purses his lips.

"Anyway, I was certain my dad was going to show up for some big reunion in front of the entire school any time we had an assembly or basketball game or play. It made me so nervous I'd spend all day throwing up in the bathroom. I talked Maria Carmen and Talib into coming in here with me so I wouldn't have to sit through the assembly. I didn't feel like barfing all day."

Miss Humala's hard expression softens, and she

sighs. "Well, all right. But you really shouldn't be in here unsupervised."

We nod enthusiastically and head for the door.

"Did you find what you were looking for?" Miss Humala asks behind us.

"What?" Maria Carmen spins around, smacking Talib and me with her braids.

"The trivia cards. Did you find them?" Miss Humala asks, walking over to the filing cabinet behind her desk.

"Oh, no. We didn't."

Miss Humala opens the top drawer of the cabinet and pulls out a stack of cards from a folder. She holds them out to me, and I move to take them, hoping she can't see my hand shaking.

"These cards are advanced, but I think you all can handle them," Miss Humala says. She doesn't let go of the cards despite my trying to take them. She leans in closer and whispers, "I'd strongly advise you against wandering alone where you shouldn't."

My breath catches in my throat, and I cough. Miss Humala releases the cards from her red talons, and I slip them into my pocket.

"Thanks," I mumble as we rush out the door.

"I think I need to go home and change my shorts," Talib says as we walk down the hallway to our next class.

As we sit later in history class, ignoring Mr. Gearhart as he drones on about the Battle of San Jacinto, Maria Carmen leans in close to me. "Was that true? What you told Miss Humala?"

I continue filling in the scales of the snake I'm drawing in my sketchbook, making sure to get just the right shade of "I will pop your eyeballs out in your sleep."

"Yeah, it is."

Talib nudges me. "I always thought those reunion videos were cool. I never figured they'd make someone sad."

I shrug. "They *are* cool, don't get me wrong. It's just that when I was little, I never knew if my mom and I were going to a baseball game or going to see Dad. Going out for ice cream or going to see Dad."

"Going to get a root canal. Going to see your dad," Talib offers.

"Exactly."

"That would drive me nuts," Maria Carmen says.

Mr. Gearhart clears his throat from the front of the

classroom, and we hunch over our desks, pretending to scribble notes.

The bell mercifully rings, and we gather our things.

"Well, I guess we didn't figure out anything about the witch," Maria Carmen says. "Miss Humala's classroom was a bust."

"Other than giving me an ulcer," Talib says.

"I still think she has something to do with it," I say, walking down the hall. I'm not sure how to tell them that Milla confessed to Miss Humala's conversations with a snake.

Passing Miss Humala's classroom, I peek inside and spot her sitting behind her desk at the front of the room. Her head is lowered, and she's staring at the floor next to her.

"Hold up," I whisper to Talib and Maria Carmen. They stand behind me as I peer around the doorframe. "I think she's talking to someone."

I look on the floor next to her desk and spot a coil of brown scales. "Or some*thing*," I add.

"What's she saying?" Talib whispers behind me.

I wave him to be quiet and listen in.

"I came here to get away from you. To get away from

what you did last time. Why'd you have to follow me?" Miss Humala whispers.

There's a loud thud on the side of her desk. I squint and see a tail slither around Miss Humala's ankle.

"You have to be more careful. You're just causing too many problems," Miss Humala says to the snake. "They're going to find out about you, Mother."

Mother?

CHAPTER 16

I'VE TRACED OVER *DEAR DAD* so many times on the page of my sketchbook I've punched my pencil through the words. Recent events in New Haven definitely don't fit Mom's Always Be Positive, Always Be Happy rule.

I give it my best shot.

Dear Dad,

We won our first trivia club match! Maria Carmen, Talib, and I are studying super-hard animal facts so we can really crush it next time. I'm definitely going to stump you now. For example . . .

This amphibian gives birth to fully formed offspring . . . through its mouth!

Yeah, Talib threw up after learning this one.

I found some Hot Wheels in the back of my closet last week. One of them was black, but someone had taken red nail polish and written "RAL" on both sides. You need to work on your paint-job skills, Dad. I may have added some flames to the top of it, but they're purple because that's the only nail polish color Abuela has. It still looks good.

Love you. Stay safe.
Nestor

Trivia club. My dad's old toys.

Always Be Positive. Always Be Happy.

Someday I might figure out how to let Dad know what really goes on with me while he's far away. How to let him still be Dad instead of just a pen pal.

"You know, they have this amazing invention called email that lets you send messages instantly across the world," Talib tells me, raising an eyebrow and pointing to my letter. He leans in closer and scans my words. "Hey. I did *not* throw up."

"You turned as green as the Darwin's frog from the video we were watching."

"Well, yeah. But, c'mon, man. Babies. Out of its *mouth*." Talib shudders.

Maria Carmen clears her throat and taps her fork on the cafeteria table. We're ignoring the limp spaghetti and shriveled boiled carrots on our trays.

I really need to start bringing my lunch.

"If it's not too much trouble, guys, do you think we should discuss the pesky little problem of the witch in the woods and the fact that it's Miss Humala's mom?" she asks, tossing her braids behind her shoulders.

"And that other little, tiny side note of our friend Brandon working for the witch," I add.

Talib sighs, poking a mushy carrot with his fork. "Sixth grade. What a breeze."

I look over at the corner of the cafeteria and spy Brandon sitting by himself, stabbing his spaghetti noodles with more enthusiasm than makes me comfortable.

"Why do I think he wishes those were live squirrels on his tray?" I ask.

Maria Carmen shakes her head. "So do you think the witch, or Miss Humala's mom, or whoever she is, asked him to do anything else?"

I push around the noodles on my tray until they resemble a snake. "There's only one way to find out."

Talib lowers his forehead onto the sticky cafeteria table. "Please don't say go in the woods. Please don't say go in the woods."

I slap Talib on the back. "We have to go in the woods."

"I hate my life."

Cuervito soars above us as we meander down the trail through the woods, swooping in close and making us duck.

"What'cha doin'? Huh?" he squawks as he dive-bombs my ear.

I swat him away. I want to ask Cuervito if he's seen anything suspicious in the woods, but Maria Carmen and Talib follow me too closely.

"So what exactly are we looking for?" Maria Carmen asks, kicking a rock down the path.

I shrug. "I don't know. More traps?"

A squirrel runs across the path in front of me and asks, "Field trip?"

I shake my head.

Talib looks behind us. "Are we sure there's . . . nothing else out here with us?"

I point to the squirrel still sitting in front of me. "I don't know. Let's ask," I joke. "Hey, squirrel, you wouldn't happen to have seen a witch running around here, terrorizing your fellow woodland creatures?"

Maria Carmen and Talib look at me funny, and I laugh weakly.

The squirrel stares at me. "She's everywhere. Behind every tree, under every rock."

I give a small nod and swallow hard. Throwing up my hands, I tell Maria Carmen and Talib, "Well, he's no help."

Maria Carmen shakes her head at me. "Keep looking for traps, Nestor."

We look under every live oak and cedar tree, every mesquite bush, every cactus. All we find is one more trap of Brandon's that we missed before.

"Do you think the witch is done? Maybe she's

leaving," Talib says, putting the coils from Brandon's trap into his pocket.

"I don't think so," I tell him. "When she was talking to Miss Humala, it sounded like she was still up to something. And have you seen all the missing-pet signs in town?"

Talib nods. "You can't even see any of the windows downtown anymore. They're all plastered."

"Well, now what? How are we going to keep all these animals safe? How are we going to stop everyone in town from thinking your abuela is involved?" Maria Carmen sighs as she sits down on a fallen tree trunk.

"I don't think you guys are going to like this idea, but . . ." I pause, wondering how Maria Carmen and Talib are going to take what I'm about to say.

"Oh, Nestor, don't say it," Talib mumbles, head in his hands as he sits next to Maria Carmen.

"We need to talk to Brandon," I tell them.

Maria Carmen purses her lips and nods.

Talib won't look at me. "Or we could jump into a volcano. Or swim with genetically mutated zombie sharks."

Maria Carmen nudges Talib with her elbow. I put

my hand on his shoulder. "Don't worry, Talib. It'll be fine. We won't let anything happen to you."

Talib looks up at me and smiles. He sticks out his chin and bats his long black eyelashes. "Just promise this cute face won't get messed up."

I lightly slap his cheek. "Let's go."

We head down the trail, over a hill, and around a patch of mesquite bushes. The sun lowers in the sky, dipping behind the quarry to the west.

"Quick question. Do either of you know where Brandon lives?" I ask.

Maria Carmen and Talib look at each other and shrug.

"Seriously?" I say. "This town could fit on a mosquito's back."

They shrug again.

We continue down the trail heading toward our houses, still as lost as when we first entered the woods. I kick a rock in frustration, sending it rolling down the dirt.

We're almost at a full century cactus, the point where we usually split up, when I hear a shout coming from the bottom of the next hill.

"Nestor! Nestor! Where are you?"

I recognize the voice.

Chela the deer comes running at us, hooves pounding into the dirt, nostrils flaring.

"Nestor, watch out!" Maria Carmen shouts.

We jump off the trail, but Chela skids to a stop directly in front of us.

"Nestor, it's your grandmother," she says. "You have to come with me. She's hurt."

CHAPTER 17

"ABUELA'S HURT?" I ASK CHELA. "Where is she?"

"The woods just past your house. Not far," she replies, turning around and taking off down the trail. "Hurry!"

I run after Chela, my heart pounding and my feet sliding on the rocky hills.

I don't notice Maria Carmen and Talib running behind me until I hear Maria Carmen shout, "Nestor! Where are you going? What happened?"

I can't answer her now. I have to find Abuela. I have to help her.

Spotting Abuela's house in the distance, I search the woods. There's a mesquite bush that looks like a wrecking ball hit it. The branch of a cedar tree lies smashed on the ground. A cactus has been slashed to ribbons, long claw marks scarring its flesh.

Chela skids behind a tree and says, "Here, Nestor. She's here."

Running to where Chela is standing, I spot Abuela on the ground, her back against a twisting live oak tree. Scratched in the bark above her are three long, jagged lines. Her chest heaves slowly as she struggles to breathe. A small trickle of blood snakes down from her forehead and into her eye.

"Buela!" I can hardly hear my own voice over my heartbeat pounding in my ears.

Abuela lifts her hand slowly out to me. "Ay, mi niño. You found me. You found me. That's good . . ."

Her voice trails off, and her eyelids slowly droop.

My throat tightens as I crouch down next to her and put my hands on her shoulders.

"Oh my gosh, Señora Lopez," Maria Carmen says behind me. She crouches on the other side and brushes Abuela's hair from her forehead.

Abuela winces. "Ese maldito ratón." She lets loose a

string of curses that makes Maria Carmen and I blush. Talib stands behind us, oblivious to Abuela's verbal assault.

"Is she okay?" he asks.

"I don't know," I tell him. Abuela's cheeks are flushed red, and a nasty gash crosses her forehead. She's holding her left arm and flinches when I touch it.

Abuela draws in a deep breath. "Gracias. Gracias, mi amiguita. I knew you would find him."

I realize Abuela is talking to Chela, who's still standing behind us. "Buela, can you understand her, too?"

Abuela sighs and lifts her hand to my cheek. "Mi niño, mi niño, I knew you had it. I always knew you had it."

My chin quivers as I cover Abuela's hand with my own.

"Señora Lopez? Do you think you can stand up?" Maria Carmen asks.

Abuela nods, and Talib, Maria Carmen, and I gather around to help her up. We make slow progress to the house, Abuela leaning on Talib's and my shoulders as Maria Carmen kicks rocks and branches out of our way.

The back door of the house hangs open, and in the

kitchen, a chair is overturned, one of the legs snapped from the seat. Abuela's sewing machine lies smashed next to it, and a pair of Mom's light-green scrubs, torn to pieces, is scattered on the kitchen floor. We pass through to the living room and slowly lower Abuela onto the couch.

"There's a first aid kit upstairs in the bathroom," I tell Maria Carmen. "Can you go get it?"

She runs up the stairs as I get a wet cloth from the kitchen. I press it to Abuela's forehead, and she inhales quickly. "Y Celia? Dónde está Celia?"

Talib looks around the living room. "Who's Celia?"

I hold Abuela's hand. "What are you talking about, Buela?"

An orange tabby cat meanders from underneath the coffee table and I jump. I didn't think Abuela had a cat. "Is she okay?" the cat asks.

"I think so," I respond. "Did you see what happened?"

Maria Carmen comes down from the bathroom and hands me the first aid kit. Talib leans over to her and whispers, "First, Nestor was talking to the deer, and now he's talking to this cat. Can somebody explain what's going on?"

I wipe the blood from Abuela's forehead and examine the cut. It's not very deep, but it runs the length of her hairline. Something took a swipe at her. Something with claws.

"Is she going to be okay?" Maria Carmen asks. "Do you think we need to take her to the hospital?"

"Ay, no. No hospital. Your mami is there," Abuela says. "If she worries, your papi worries."

I have to agree with Abuela. Telling Dad his mother got attacked in the woods would definitely violate Mom's Always Be Positive, Always Be Happy rule.

"I'll just put some Vivaporú on it." A small smile creeps from the corner of Abuela's mouth.

"Abuela, you are not putting Vicks VapoRub on a cut." I can't help but roll my eyes at Abuela's complete faith in dubious Cuban remedies.

The orange tabby cat rubs against my leg, her purring numbing my tense muscles. "Your grandma always treats me nice with leftover croquetas and the best guava slices. All the other neighbors around here just ignore the stray cat. So I tried to help her. I tried to stop the wolverine. But it was too quick."

"A wolverine? In the house?"

"It came through the back door while your abuela

and I were watching novelas." The cat nudges Abuela's hand, and Abuela scratches her furry head.

"Ay, mi Celia. Always looking out for me," Abuela says.

Maria Carmen crouches next to Abuela. She cleans Abuela's cut with the wet cloth and puts antibacterial cream on it. My hands are still shaking too much to be useful.

Talib hands a bandage to Maria Carmen. "Nestor, I'm assuming when all this is over, you're going to explain how you're talking to animals. Right?"

I lower my head. Abuela chuckles from the couch. "Es bendecido. Igual como yo."

"I'm blessed?" I ask Abuela. Being able to talk to and hear animals never really felt like a blessing.

Suddenly, everything begins to make sense. I think back to the times I heard Abuela arguing with someone who wasn't there. The whole time, it's been this stray cat rubbing against my leg. I remember Dad's animal encyclopedia with the weird notes next to his drawings. *Mami says squirrels tell the best knock-knock jokes. According to Mami, hedgehogs think prairie dogs are obnoxious.* There's only one way Abuela could've known those things.

Maria Carmen secures a bandage to Abuela's forehead, and Abuela smiles. "Si, mi niño. When your papi couldn't hear them, I thought maybe it was just me. But you, I knew you were just like me."

Tears well up in my eyes as Abuela squeezes my hand.

Maria Carmen clears her throat. "Señora Lopez, what did the wolverine want?"

Abuela sighs. "Ese estúpido ratón."

Talib chuckles behind me. "I gotta write these down."

"She was angry that you three destroyed her traps. That I've been helping animals get away from her. She was so angry," Abuela says, touching the bandage on her forehead and closing her eyes.

"Do you know what she wants? What she is?" I ask.

Abuela sits up on the couch, and Maria Carmen sets two pillows next to her to lean on. "She's like a tule vieja, I think."

"A tule what?" Talib asks.

"Tule vieja. A witch. When I was little, my papi would tell me ghost stories, monster stories, any kind of scary story. Mami hated it because sometimes they gave me nightmares. But I loved it. I remember Papi telling me the story of the tule vieja from Panama. She was a woman who had the legs of a hawk, the wings of a bat, and the face of an old witch. I was convinced the rooster that lived in our backyard was a tule vieja after it tried to bite my thumb off."

Abuela shifts her weight on the couch and draws in a slow breath. "But this one is different. A tule vieja just looks like different animals. She can't completely turn *into* an animal. This one is trying to take the animal's power."

"How does she do that?" Maria Carmen asks.

"She bites them."

Talib swallows hard.

I think about all the animals that have gone missing without a single trace. A single piece of evidence. I can't help but wonder if the tule vieja is doing more than just biting them.

"When she came here, she didn't realize what Nestor and I could do. That we could use our ability to help the animals escape her. Her plan is harder with us here."

"What's her plan?" I ask.

"The eclipse," Abuela says, her breathing slowing and her shoulders sagging. "If she wants to turn into an animal, she has to bite them during the eclipse. Right now, she can only turn into a snake, a wolverine, and a spider. Those are probably the animals she bit during another eclipse."

Talib's head snaps up. "Excuse me? A spider?"

"So the eclipse will help her or something?" I ask.

"Yes. If she bites an animal during the eclipse, she'll be able to turn into that animal. She'll be even more powerful."

"How do you know all this, Buela?" I ask.

Abuela taps her temple with a shaking finger. "Bueno, all that stomping around in the woods, you see things. More things than you wanted to see."

She takes a deep breath and stretches her back, groaning. "And la estúpida talks to herself. All this going on and on about the eclipse. Enough tontería to make animals want to disappear all on their own."

Maria Carmen covers her mouth to hide her smile.

Abuela sighs, and I help her lie down on the couch again. Her eyelids close, and soon her breaths come in rhythmic waves.

Maria Carmen, Talib, and I head into the kitchen. I straighten the fallen chair, finding the snapped leg under the table, and attempt to fix it. Maria Carmen sets Abuela's sewing machine back on the table and throws away the shredded pieces of Mom's scrubs.

Gripping the chair, I look at Maria Carmen and Talib. "So I guess you guys think I'm super weird now."

Talib comes over to me and slaps me on the shoulder. "Oh, no. We thought that way before now. Who else knows more about the military than our history teacher and carries a compass to walk three blocks?"

Maria Carmen chuckles. "But seriously, Nestor. You can really talk to animals? And they talk back to you?"

I shrug, not wanting to look them in the eye. "Yeah. I guess."

Maria Carmen crosses her arms. "Prove it. How do we know you aren't just making up what that cat and deer said?"

I scuff my foot on the tile floor and look at Maria Carmen. The glint in her eye makes me smirk. "Well, let's just say a certain raven told me that sometimes you stop at the skate park on your way home, and when you think no one's watching, you belt out Selena songs. Complete with dance moves."

Maria Carmen's cheeks flush red, and Talib cackles next to her.

"And you," I say, pointing to him. The smile

disappears from his face. "That same raven has peeked in your window and seen that you still sleep with a stuffed llama."

"Hey! Don't make fun of Mr. Fuzzbuns," Talib says, hands on hips.

"Okay, that's awesome," Maria Carmen says.

"Sometimes it is. But sometimes it's really annoying."

"Really?" Talib asks.

"Yeah. I had lice in the first grade. Hundreds of voices yelling at me all at once. Worst weekend ever," I say, shaking my head.

Talib slaps me on the back and laughs.

We walk back to the living room, and I peek over the back of the couch at Abuela. My abuela, who was strong enough to start over in a new country all by herself, whose laughter fills up every corner of the kitchen as she makes the best Cuban food I've ever tasted. My abuela, who dances to Celia Cruz while she tells me about the latest episode of her favorite telenovela. My abuela, who can talk to animals, sinks her head farther into the pillow and sleeps.

CHAPTER 18

Dear Dad,

Things are still good here in New Haven. Mom seems to like her job at the hospital in Springdale.

But sometimes I hear her cry at night when she thinks I've already fallen asleep. She misses you a lot.

School is fine. Our trivia team is still doing well. We might even make it to the championship.

If we're still living here and

haven't moved to Alaska or
Antarctica.

It's been nice living with Abuela.
She lets me have pastelitos for
breakfast and dinner. And as an
after-school snack. Don't tell Mom.
Although she'll probably find out
eventually when she has to buy me
larger pants.

Abuela got hurt last week. We
didn't tell Mom, so Abuela just
pretended to have a cold and slept
in her room all day. She pinned some
of her hair in front of the cut along
her forehead so Mom wouldn't see it.
I don't like seeing how slowly Abuela
moves around the kitchen. She didn't
used to do that.

Love you. Stay safe.

I miss you, Dad. I don't want you
far away anymore. I want you here.
It's not fair that I have to figure
everything out on my own.

I need my dad. I need you.

Nestor

I slam my sketchbook closed, frustrated that I can't tell Dad what I really need to say to him. I'm tired of Mom's Always Be Positive, Always Be Happy rule.

Miss Humala's sharp voice snaps me from my thoughts. "Solar eclipses aren't as uncommon as you might think. The moon will cross a point between Earth and the sun one or two times every thirty-five days."

She stands behind three students she's pulled to the front of the classroom. They're each holding a model of Earth, the moon, or the sun. Miss Humala has Jet, the boy holding the model of Earth, walk slowly around Hannah, the girl holding the model of the sun. She has Leif, the boy holding the model of the moon, walk quickly around Jet. He starts to look dizzy.

"So as you can see," Miss Humala says as Jet, Hannah, and Leif continue to orbit around one another, "it looks like we would experience a solar eclipse any time the moon is between Earth and the sun."

She stops Leif, who seems grateful to not be pacing in a circle anymore, and he stands between Jet and Hannah. "But Earth and the moon don't orbit at a constant level."

Miss Humala digs her red talons into Leif's

shoulders and pushes down on him. He groans and bends his knees. Then she grabs his biceps and pulls him up. Miss Humala walks Leif around Jet, pushing and pulling on him. He bends and straightens his knees, moving the moon in a wobbly orbit around Earth.

I think he might throw up.

Miss Humala switches over to Jet, who looks increasingly nervous, and pushes and pulls on him as well. She drags him around Hannah all while Leif is still circling Jet.

It's like a bad carnival ride.

"Remind me to never volunteer in this class," I whisper to Talib.

"So, Earth and the moon are always moving up and down in their orbit," Miss Humala says as Jet and Leif continue walking in a circle, bending and straightening their knees. Their faces turn pink, and I can see sweat forming on their foreheads.

She stops Leif, who sighs, between Jet and Hannah. "Because of this, Earth, the moon, and the sun will only line up perfectly to form a solar eclipse about twice a year."

Jet, Leif, and Hannah give their models back to Miss Humala and return to their seats. Leif drops his head on his desk with a groan. I scan Miss Humala's face for any sign that she knows what we're up to. That we know what her mother is doing. But she's busy passing out a worksheet on solar eclipses.

"Are you ready for a really awkward trivia competition?" Talib whispers to me.

"Miss Humala, Brandon, and the three of us all in the auditorium after school? Yeah, it's gonna be great," I say.

Maria Carmen turns and whispers, "Neither of you think it's weird that Miss Humala is teaching us about solar eclipses today?"

I shrug. "It's probably just because one is coming up."

I stare at Miss Humala as she towers over a student and glares because he forgot to put his name on his worksheet. She's canceled our last three trivia club practices. Most of the time, she just stands by the window in her classroom, staring into the woods.

Yesterday I spotted a spiderweb tangled in her hair.

"It's been seven years since the continental United

States saw a total solar eclipse," Miss Humala continues. "The next one will occur in five days and will pass directly through central Texas."

I think about what Abuela told us about the tule vieja, or whatever Miss Humala's mother really is. She said that the witch is most powerful during the eclipse. That means in five days, all the animals in the woods and in New Haven will be in danger.

We have to do something.

But first we have a trivia competition to win.

Talib keeps pulling on the collar of his shirt, mirroring a student from Crockett Middle School in Austin across from us—his tie looks like it's a second away from strangling him to death. The three other students from Crockett look annoyed to be spending time in a town like New Haven. I guess they'd rather be back in Austin forming a band. Or starting their own tech companies. I wonder if Crockett forces its kids to join the quiz team instead of doing detention.

"This animal defecates on itself to keep cool and will vomit as a defense mechanism," the quiz bowl moderator says.

Talib buzzes in and shouts, "Turkey vulture." He

winks at his parents, sitting in the front row of the auditorium. Talib's mom gives him a wide smile, and his dad holds out a thumbs-up.

I mutter a quick prayer that no turkey vultures are in the woods for the tule vieja to bite. No way am I going up against a pooping, barfing witch.

The moderator awards us 100 points, and Talib and I smile at each other as we answer the bonus question correctly as well. Our team is doing great, thanks to Brandon keeping silent. His face is as white as an albino alligator, and he's bitten all his nails down to nubs.

The moderator, the same high-pants-wearing man from our first competition, clears his throat into the microphone and knocks on the podium with his knobby hands.

"Children, this light-sensitive animal, native to the lakes and rivers of Mexico, can regenerate limbs and even body organs," Mr. Highpants breathes into the microphone.

Maria Carmen buzzes in and says, "Axolotl."

Her mom claps from the front row. I pretend not to see her scowl at me directly after as Talib answers the bonus question.

"Well done, New Haven. You are up two hundred sixty to zero," Mr. Highpants says, holding up a new card. "Next question. This primate can catch human colds and other illnesses."

Maria Carmen and Talib search each other's faces as if the answer might be written on a pimple somewhere. Brandon chews on the drawstring of his hoodie while the team from Crockett pulls on their ties. One of the girls has managed to twirl her frizzy hair so tightly around her finger, it's gotten stuck. They won't be buzzing in any time soon.

I hit the buzzer in front of me. "Gorillas."

No one is in the front row of the auditorium to give me a thumbs-up.

"I thought your abuela was going to come," Maria Carmen whispers next to me while Mr. Highpants awards us more points.

"She wanted to. But I told her if she still wasn't feeling well, she should rest," I say.

With Dad always gone and Mom working long hours, I'm used to being on my own at school functions. That doesn't stop me from scanning every chair in the auditorium.

The competition proceeds, and we continue to

trounce Crockett. They do manage to answer one question correctly when Tie Boy accidentally hits the buzzer trying to smash a gnat flying around his table. He mumbles, "Annoying gnat," which happens to be the answer to "Which insect has hairlike antennae and is known for causing fungus in mushrooms and the roots of potted plants?"

Mr. Highpants doesn't even bother facing the Crockett team anymore and directs the last question to us. "During World War II, Americans tried to train this type of animal to drop bombs."

Maria Carmen and Talib shrug and look at me. Brandon's knee bounces up and down as he gnaws on his thumbnail.

I raise my arm high in the air and bring my hand smashing down on the buzzer.

"Bats!"

Thanks, Dad.

We gather onstage after the competition. Miss Humala congratulates us briefly before hurrying out the back doors behind the stage. I raise my eyebrows at Talib, and he shrugs. Brandon shuffled out of the auditorium the moment the competition was over. Maria Carmen's mom gives her a kiss on the cheek and tells her, "Felicidades, mija!" Talib's parents ask Maria Carmen to take a picture of them with Talib, the three of them smiling broadly.

And I stand there with my hands in my pockets.

When I was in first grade, at Fort Benning in Georgia, my school had a Donuts with Dad event every month. I'd spend the morning sitting with Andre, whose dad died before he was born, and Isabel, whose dad moved to Argentina after her parents divorced. They'd both give me sympathetic smiles that made me want to shout that I had a dad who was alive and well and loved me. Eventually, I just sat by myself.

Maria Carmen turns to me, flipping her braids. "Mami and I are going to the pharmacy for ice cream. Wanna come?"

Before I can respond, Ms. Cordova puts her hand on Maria Carmen's shoulder. "I'm sure he has better things to do, mija."

The way her lips press into a tight line and her eyes narrow tells me I should turn down this particular invitation.

I scuff my feet on the stage floor. "That's okay. I need to get home to Abuela."

Maria Carmen shrugs and mouths "sorry" to me as she and her mother leave.

Talib shuffles over to me and mumbles, "I wanted to invite you over, but my parents said no." He won't look me in the eye.

"It's my abuela, isn't it? They think she has something to do with all the missing animals, too?"

"Yeah. Sorry."

I slap him lightly on the arm. "It's okay. I get it," I lie.

Talib steps in closer to me and whispers, "We'll get that tule vieja, Nestor. Don't worry. We'll get her, and then people will see that your grandma is innocent."

I smile at Talib and head out of the auditorium.

I've never stayed anywhere long enough for people to form an opinion of me. By the time they decide my obsession with Pokémon cards is weird, I'm already packing my bags.

But it also means I've never had to stay somewhere long enough to endure people hating me.

CHAPTER 19

"WHY SO BUMMED, KID? You look like someone pooped on your Pringles," Cuervito says as he soars above me.

"You want a list?" I kick an acorn across the trail through the woods.

"Bring it."

I hold up my fingers. "There's a witch stealing all the animals in town. Everybody thinks it's my abuela. My friends' parents hate me. My dad is thousands of miles away. And I'm probably going to have to move again in a few months. Is that enough for you?"

Cuervito glides down and lands on the path in front of me. "Huh. Yeah, I think I'd be bummed, too." He hops slowly across the path and lowers his head. "In fact, I'm feeling pretty sad right now."

I smirk and shake my head. "You'll get over it."

"Nope. Not with that crazy witch in the woods. She wants to pluck my feathers and boil me for dinner!"

I take Dad's compass out of my pocket and rub my thumb over its face.

"Your dad's, right?" the raven asks.

"Yeah. I wish he were here. He'd know what to do." I watch the needle swing back and forth until it rests on north. "Maybe it'll point to the tule vieja."

Cuervito tilts his head at the compass. "It should point at the best roadkill."

"You're disgusting."

A twig snaps behind us, and I jerk my head to scan the trees. Each time I walk through the woods, I notice more claw slashes on tree trunks and more smashed cacti.

"How about more walking, less talking. Yeah?" Cuervito says, and I quicken my pace home.

We crest the hill and head down into Abuela's

backyard. Mom comes out onto the porch, her arms outstretched.

"There you are! How was the competition? I bet you trounced them," she says, a huge grin on her face.

I nod and smile, giving her a hug.

"Victory selfie before I have to go!" Mom says, holding out her phone. She snaps a quick photo that cuts off our foreheads.

"Where are you going?" I ask, shoving my hands into my pockets.

Mom slides her phone into the back pocket of her jeans. "Nursing conference in Dallas. First time I'm going to one. It's exciting!"

She gives me another hug, and I don't let go. I'm used to Dad being the one that leaves. This is the first time Mom has ever gone somewhere without me.

Mom breaks our hug and looks me in the eyes. "Hey, you'll be fine. You're the man of the house now, right? Take care of your abuela for me."

Giving me a quick kiss on the cheek, Mom heads back into the house. I slump down on the porch steps and pick at the hem of my shirt.

I scan the edge of Abuela's backyard and spot the

strangest parade marching toward me: Val, Chela with her fawn, and three squirrels, all looking at me.

"Is there a convention in town I don't know about?" I ask Cuervito as he sails down and hops next to me.

He squawks. "It's a 'there's a witch in the woods and we need your help' convention."

I get up and walk over to Chela. She nods. "Hello, Nestor."

"Hi," I say. "So thanks for helping my abuela the other day. I didn't get to say that . . . with everything going on."

"You're very welcome, and now we need your help," Chela says. "Something has to be done. Your grandmother was doing what she could for us, but now she can't help. And I'm afraid helping cost her too much. We've heard a lot of talk from the people in town about her. They think she's responsible for all the missing animals. They don't realize that she was only helping us."

"What was she doing?"

"She was giving us places to hide, marking those traps that vile boy set."

Val hops up to me. "Thanks for getting rid of those, by the way."

I look at the coyote's back leg. A red scar circles it just above his foot. "Glad to see you're doing better."

The squirrels scamper over one another. "Gotta get rid of the witch. Gotta get rid of the witch."

"What is she exactly?" Chela asks.

"Oh, I know this one! I know this!" Cuervito screeches. "She's a turnip violet. No, she's a toilet vittle. Yep, that's it. Toilet vittle."

I shake my head. "She's a tule vieja. She bites animals so she can get their powers and turn into them."

Cuervito bobs his beak up and down. "Yep. Just like I said."

The tumble of squirrel fur shouts, "Don't like that! Nope, definitely don't like that!"

"So how do we stop her?" Chela asks, inching closer to her fawn.

"I'm figuring that out," I tell her. "Whatever we do, we have to do it soon, though. My abuela says she'll be able to turn into any animal she bites during the solar eclipse."

"When's the eclipse?" Val asks.

"In five days."

The animals stare at me. I know they're waiting for

me to tell them my brilliant plan to stop the tule vieja for good.

But I have nothing.

I feel a sharp smack on the back of my head and see an acorn roll on the ground next to me.

"Intruder!" Cuervito cries, flapping his wings and flying into the air.

I turn to see Brandon stomping down the hill toward Abuela's backyard. He reaches down and picks up another acorn, launching it at me, and I duck, the acorn bouncing off Chela's side.

"What is your problem?" I shout, searching the yard for something I can throw back at him.

Val scampers in front of me. "Don't worry, Nestor. We got you."

Cuervito soars above Brandon. "I pooped on you once, kid. I'll do it again!"

Brandon runs closer to me, his face pale. He's got dark circles under his eyes and scratches along his arms. "Stop. You have to stop," he mumbles as he enters the yard.

Val lunges at him, snapping his small, sharp teeth. Cuervito swoops down, brushing the top of Brandon's head with his wings.

This breaks Brandon out of his trance. He blinks and shakes his head.

"Nestor, you have to stay away from the witch."

"No way. She hurt my abuela. And she's going to do a lot worse if we don't do something about it."

Brandon stomps his foot on the ground. "You have to stop looking for her. I told her I wouldn't help her anymore, and then . . . she . . ."

"What?"

"*She took my dad.*"

CHAPTER 20

"IF I WANTED TO BE IN A GROUP with the world's worst person," Maria Carmen hisses at me, "I would've asked Brandon to join us. Oh, wait. You already did."

She narrows her eyes as Brandon sinks lower in his chair. He pulls his ratty fatigue-green jacket tight around him, his knuckles as white as his face.

"Group work is one thing, Nestor, but c'mon," Talib says, pulling his desk next to mine. Maria Carmen shoves her desk next to Brandon's, our four desks making a square.

Miss Humala stands at the front of the room,

pointing to a map of Texas projected on the board. "Make sure you label each section of the state with the percentage of eclipse totality. Then, for our area, label the time for the phases of the eclipse."

I notice a bandage wrapped around her arm and wonder if it's covering a wolverine slash—just like the one on my abuela's forehead.

Maria Carmen, Talib, and I huddle over our map. Brandon chews on his fingernail.

"Look, I get it. We don't have the best history," I tell them.

"Try World War III with pudding and rocks," Talib snorts.

Brandon mumbles under his breath, "I had to."

Maria Carmen's head snaps in his direction. "You were a jerk long before this tule vieja came into town, and you know it."

Brandon's mouth drops open as if he were about to say something, but he ends up just staring at her.

Miss Humala claps as she stands by the window at the back of the classroom. Her eyes dart toward the woods. "This is due at the end of class, so make sure you're working diligently."

Talib rolls his eyes and slides our paper onto his

desk, beginning to fill out how much of the eclipse each part of Texas will be able to see. New Haven is directly in the path of the total solar eclipse.

"Yes, he's been a jerk. He won't deny it," I say, pointing at Brandon. He purses his lips and nods. "But this is different. His dad is gone. The tule vieja took him."

Maria Carmen's eyebrows scrunch together. She grips her pencil so tightly it starts to crack. "How long have you been on your own?"

Brandon sighs, and his stomach grumbles loudly. "Four days."

Talib stops writing on our paper and looks at Brandon. For a moment, I think he's going to reach out and put his hand on Brandon's arm, but he presses his hands on his desk instead.

Miss Humala hovers over our desks. "Busy at work?" she says, raising her eyebrow into a pointed arch.

Maria Carmen flips a braid over her shoulder and clears her throat. "Miss Humala, is it true that some cultures think that eclipses have special powers?"

I dig my fingernails into my palms. I'm certain Miss Humala is aware we know her mother is the tule vieja. Maria Carmen needs to be more careful.

Miss Humala gives a strained laugh. "Oh, dear. This is science class. That's a better question for Ms. Cheng in English class. You know, for when you read mythology. Or fairy tales."

She grips the back of Talib's chair, her red fingernails digging into the hard plastic. "You know, Principal Jelani's rule about students not going in the woods is still in effect. Make sure you're following it."

The group next to us starts arguing about how long the total eclipse will be visible in New Haven, and Miss Humala snaps from the death stare she's giving us to walk over to them.

"Next time, why don't you just ask her where her mother is and how we can stop her," Talib mumbles, head in his hands.

A smile creeps from the corner of Brandon's mouth.

"We need to figure out two things," I tell them.

"What's that?" Maria Carmen asks.

"Where Miss Humala's mother is. And how we can stop her."

Talib slams his forehead down on his desk.

A chuckle erupts from Brandon's throat, and we stare at him. He looks at us and shakes his head. "She's hiding in the quarry. That's where she took my dad."

"Did you see her?" Maria Carmen asks.

Brandon shoves his hands into the pockets of his jacket. "Yeah, I ran after them. But then this stupid raven stopped me. Almost pecked my eyes out."

"How did she take your dad?" I ask. I try to imagine a snake or a wolverine carrying a grown man through the woods, but I just can't.

Brandon leans forward and starts to gnaw on another nail, only to realize he's bitten every single one down to a nub. He shoves his hand back into his pocket. "Dad always has to leave for work at the oil field piping plant about an hour after dinner because he works the night shift. He hadn't left yet, so I went to check on him in the living room, and I found him sitting in his recliner with a huge red welt on his neck. His eyes were frozen open, and he wasn't moving."

Brandon shakes his head as if he's trying to fling the memory out of his ears. "There was . . . a spider. And Dad was wrapped in spider silk. Before I could try to get him out of it, something—a wolverine—slammed into me and scratched my arms. It grabbed the cocoon with its teeth and dragged my dad out of the house."

Brandon bites his lip so hard small droplets of blood form at the edge of his mouth.

Talib reaches out and puts his hand on Brandon's shoulder. "We'll get him back. Don't worry."

Maria Carmen takes our paper from Talib. "The eclipse is tomorrow. We have to get to the quarry, get Brandon's dad, and figure out how to get rid of the tule vieja."

"I don't suppose we can convince Miss Humala and her mother to move out of town," Talib mutters. "I hear Miami's nice. Or Madagascar."

"My abuela can help us," I tell them. "She knows all about the tule vieja. Maybe she has some ideas on how to get rid of her."

Miss Humala clears her throat above us, and we stare at one another, unsure of how much she heard.

Waving her hand at our paper, Miss Humala says, "It looks like you all have your work cut out for you."

CHAPTER 21

"RUN THIS BRILLIANT PLAN OF YOURS by me again," Maria Carmen demands as we head through town toward Abuela's house.

We pass light poles covered with flyers for missing cats and dogs. The window of the pharmacy has a new poster offering a reward for the return of Tommy, the Raglands' prized Arabian stallion.

The tule vieja has been busy.

"It's simple. We go to my house and get some of my dad's gear. Heavy-duty flashlights. A collapsible baton. Some rope. Who knows what we'll need."

"Any chance your dad has a grenade launcher? Or a tank?" Talib asks.

I chuckle and ignore him. "Get our supplies. Ask my abuela how to get rid of the tule vieja. Go to the quarry. Get Brandon's dad."

I hear Brandon draw in a quick breath behind me. His steps quicken as he catches up to us.

Talib turns and looks at Brandon. "Any chance you have a missile launcher? You and your dad seem to have . . . stuff."

Brandon lowers his head. "No, I'm not allowed to touch that stuff without him. I wouldn't know what to do, anyway."

"Thank God," Maria Carmen mutters, scowling at Brandon.

We turn on my street and pass Mrs. Reynolds, Abuela's neighbor, standing on her front porch.

"Trixie? Here, Trixie girl. Where are you?" she calls to the black-and-white tuxedo cat that I know lives under her porch.

"RIP, Trixie," I mumble under my breath.

Heading through the front door of Abuela's house, I call out, "Buela! I'm home!"

Usually she answers right away, telling me she's in the kitchen cooking picadillo or ropa vieja, or in the dining room sewing up the latest tear in the hem of Mom's scrubs. But she doesn't answer.

"Buela?" I call out again.

When we walk into the kitchen, something isn't right. A bowl of uncooked rice is splattered across the floor, a confetti of white against the brown tile. The refrigerator door hangs open, and a carton of milk slowly drips onto the floor from punctures in the plastic.

But that doesn't scare me as much as the smear of blood on the wall by the stove, three red streaks slashing across the yellow wallpaper.

"Señora Lopez?" Maria Carmen calls behind me, her voice quivering.

Talib sucks in a sharp breath when he sees the state of the kitchen. Brandon leans against the doorframe and mumbles, "No, not again," over and over.

I push past them and race up the stairs, my heart pounding in my ears, deafening me to Maria Carmen's pleas to be careful.

I take the stairs two at a time and find my worst
fears confirmed.

Abuela is gone.

At the beginning of Dad's first deployment, Mom
accidentally left me at the grocery store. I wandered
the canned-soup aisle at the PX until I heard her frantically screaming for me. She scooped me up in her
arms, repeating, "I'm sorry, I'm sorry, I'm sorry."

Being alone now is nothing like that. For one thing,
there's a lot more thinking that I'm going to throw up.
I swallow hard as we go through the rest of the house.
The only thing I fix is a picture of Dad that was knocked
over in the living room. Maria Carmen sweeps up the
broken glass as I set the frame back on the bookshelf.

"Why are you putting paper towels over the milk
puddles?" I hear Brandon exclaim to Talib. "Shouldn't
we be out looking?"

He's right. What else can we do? I don't know where
to go. I don't know who can help.

Talib pokes his head out from the kitchen. "Nestor,
do you have a mop to clean up the blo—" He snaps his
mouth shut as Maria Carmen gives him a hard stare.
"To, uh, to clean up in here?" he stammers.

I point to the closet, and Talib grabs the mop.

Maria Carmen puts her hand on my shoulder. "Where's your mom?"

"Nursing conference in Dallas. I . . . I don't know what I'm going to tell her. How am I going to tell her?" I sink down onto the couch and put my head in my hands. I groan. "And there's no way I can tell my dad. What would I even say? 'Sorry I let your mom get dragged off by a witch'?"

Brandon comes in from the kitchen and sits next to me on the couch. Talib follows him.

"Should we go to the police?" Talib asks.

Brandon shakes his head. "That's not a good idea."

"Why not?"

"The sheriff is a terrible cop. My dad told me to never go to him if I got in trouble. Last year he shot off his own toe with his gun, and I heard he once tasered an eighty-year-old lady in the middle of the grocery store because he thought she was stealing canta-loupes."

Maria Carmen, Talib, and I stare at Brandon. This is the most he's said since we left the school. I start to laugh. Tears fill my eyes, and my stomach aches. I can't stop laughing, and the sound erupts from my throat, out of my control. I double over as the laughter turns to sobs.

Maria Carmen puts her hand on my back. "I think we should go to my house. Nestor, you can spend the night if you need to. You, too, Brandon," she says, looking him in the eyes for the first time. "We're not going to figure anything out here. Let's get your dad's supplies, and we'll figure out the rest at my house. It'll be okay."

I sigh and trudge upstairs, Talib following me. Grabbing a bag from my bedroom, I stuff into it two shirts, a pair of jeans, Dad's animal encyclopedia, and a box of tissues.

I grow more and more frustrated as I try and fail to stuff a soccer ball inside. Talib puts his hand over mine.

"Nestor, I've got this," he says gently. He takes the bag from me, removes all the excess junk, and starts packing.

He even remembers to include underwear.

CHAPTER 22

WE ALL MARCH DOWN THE STREET toward Maria Carmen's house, heads lowered, feet shuffling on the sidewalk. We pass house after house, lights off, all quiet. The people sleeping and snoring inside have no idea what's really prowling the woods, threatening to snatch them from their beds if they get in her way. My hands keep twitching, and I have to take deep breaths to try to calm down.

We're halfway to Maria Carmen's house when we hear a shout.

"Please don't do this! Please!" a woman's voice screams into the night.

We turn a corner. A glow of light comes from the edge of the woods, behind a house.

"What do you think that is?" Talib asks.

I shrug. I've got too many thoughts swirling in my head to worry about two people having an argument. In the middle of the night. At the edge of the woods.

"Just let them go! You have to let them go!" we hear the woman cry.

Maria Carmen grabs my arm. "Nestor, I think we need to see what's going on."

I shuffle behind her as we walk closer to the house. We hide behind a hedge running along the side of the house and look into the backyard. A woman crouches on her knees in front of a small fire, while another woman stands over her, pacing back and forth.

"Is that Miss Humala?" I ask, squinting.

Miss Humala trembles on the ground, wiping tears from her cheeks. The woman above her has her back to us, her wild hair glowing like a halo in the firelight.

"Please." Miss Humala shudders. "Mother, just leave."

The wild-haired woman snarls and spits. "I can't leave yet. I'm not finished."

"But you've done enough! Haven't you gotten what you wanted?"

The woman's head snaps to the sky, her hair flying in all directions. Her body shakes, and a yell bursts from her throat that echoes through the night. Her body grows impossibly long.

"What's going on?" Talib whispers next to me.

The woman morphs into an enormous brown snake, wrapping herself tightly around Miss Humala. Her scales glisten in the firelight, and she flicks her black tongue against Miss Humala's ear.

"I'm not done yet. And you will not stop me, dear daughter."

Hot liquid rises in my throat.

Brandon shakes his head. "This town is going crazy."

"You've been such a disappointment. I had great plans for us," the snake continues. Miss Humala doesn't try to squirm against the snake's tight coils. Her chin drops to her chest, and tears fall on the snake's scales. "I will never understand why you keep fighting who you really are. Why you keep running away. But know that I'm doing this, with or without you."

"Fine. Just finish it and be gone," Miss Humala mumbles.

The snake loosens her grip around Miss Humala's torso. "Very well," she says as she uncoils from Miss Humala's body.

Talib lets out a long sigh next to me. I still can't breathe. Maria Carmen grabs my hand, and we crouch down farther behind the bush.

The snake lifts her head and snaps it to either side as fur sprouts from her scales. Claws burst from her body, and the tule vieja shakes as she turns into a wolverine.

Maria Carmen squeezes my hand even harder, my knuckles cracking.

"Nestor, I think I just peed my pants a little," Talib whispers.

The wolverine scratches her long claws on the ground. "Stay out of my way. And don't let those ridiculous children get in my way, either," she sneers. Snapping at Miss Humala one last time, she trots off into the woods, enveloped by the dark night.

Miss Humala lowers her hands to the ground as soft sobs shake her shoulders.

"Should we . . . ?" Maria Carmen asks.

I shake my head. We can't let Miss Humala know what we're up to. I don't want to give her any information to tell her mother. I don't want to wait in the dark, wondering if Abuela is okay. I don't want to be lost, not knowing what to do without Dad.

We retreat from behind the bush and run the rest of the way to Maria Carmen's house, our lungs and legs aching with fear.

Maria Carmen's mother purses her lips as Maria Carmen stands in the middle of the living room, asking if we can stay over. I've never seen an eyebrow arch so high. It looks like it might disappear into her hair.

"Mami, please. We have a big trivia tournament coming up. We need an all-night study session," Maria Carmen begs. "I know it's a school night, but we promise we won't be too tired tomorrow."

Ms. Cordova draws in a long breath, and it sucks all the air from the room. She pinches her eyebrows together. "Fine. You all have sleeping bags?"

"Yes, ma'am," Talib says, holding up a sleeping bag I recognize from the boxes in my closet.

Before Ms. Cordova can interrogate us more, Maria Carmen herds us upstairs to her room. Talib, Brandon, and I stand in the center of the room, staring at shelves crammed with books and pictures. Her walls are covered with pictures of her and her brother, posters of her favorite skateboarder, and drawings of Texas wildflowers. On the nightstand next to her bed is a framed picture of Maria Carmen, her mother, and her brother in a cap and gown.

"You guys can put the bags there," Maria Carmen says, pointing to her closet.

We don't move. I don't think any of us has ever been in a girl's room before.

Maria Carmen snaps her fingers at us, and we bump into one another, throwing our bags down and sitting on the floor. I look at a large fish tank on top of Maria Carmen's bookshelf. Instead of a fish, there's a long salamander-looking creature inside, with short brown stalks growing out of its head like a crown.

"Is that an axolotl?" I ask.

Maria Carmen nods. "That's Chispa."

"He's pretty cool," Brandon offers sheepishly. He still seems nervous around Maria Carmen.

"Well, you can't hunt him," she snaps, and Brandon pulls his jacket tight around his chest.

I look at the axolotl swimming slowly in his tank. "Pero ella nunca me da de comer. Me voy a morir. En serio, hermano, ayúdame," the axolotl moans.

I double over, laughing.

"What's so funny?" Maria Carmen asks.

"Your axolotl says you never feed him and he's gonna die. He's begging me for food."

Maria Carmen marches over to the tank. "You little twerp. I feed you all the time. Don't tell lies just so you can get fat on extra food."

The axolotl flicks his tail and swims lazily under a rock.

Talib looks at me and gestures toward Brandon. "Nestor, you just gonna do your thing like that? Everybody here know about you?"

"He was having a conference with a bunch of animals in his backyard last week. Secret's out," Brandon says.

I shrug. I'm way past the point of caring what my

friends think of my ability. Finding Abuela and getting rid of the tule vieja are more important. So far, they haven't run screaming for the hills when I chat up the local wildlife, so maybe it'll be okay.

Sliding my backpack over, I pull out my sketchbook. I flip to the page where I wrote notes about the tule vieja based on what Val and Abuela told me. "All right. Let's figure out how to get rid of this witch."

We go around and around for hours. We have to stop briefly and pretend to ask one another animal-trivia questions when Ms. Cordova brings up soda and popcorn sprinkled with chili powder. Brandon eats the entire bowl. I wonder how he's been feeding himself since his dad was taken.

"So we know the tule vieja can turn into a spider, a snake, and a wolverine. Maybe we need to think about what the weakness is of each of those animals," Maria Carmen suggests.

Talib drums his fingers on his chin. "Let's see. A spider," he says, a grin growing on his face. "Maybe a shoe?"

Brandon smirks. "That's actually not a bad idea."

I shake my head. "Unless the tule vieja suddenly

changes into a wolverine and eats the shoe. And your foot."

Maria Carmen points to her laptop screen. "Check this out. What kind of spider has the strongest web? One that would be able to hold a person?"

Talib tilts his head, thinking. "I should know this one."

I give him a moment and then lean over and whisper, "Darwin's bark spider."

He snaps his fingers together. "Darwin's bark spider! See, told you I knew it."

Maria Carmen shakes her head. "Anyway, the Darwin's bark spider is native to Madagascar. And there was a solar eclipse in Madagascar eight years ago."

"So this tule vieja traveled all the way to Madagascar and chomped on a spider during a solar eclipse?" Talib asks.

"Sounds like it," Brandon replies, rubbing the back of his neck.

I write down *spider*, *Madagascar*, and *eight years ago* in my sketchbook.

"What about wolverines?" I ask. "Any eclipses lately where they're from?"

Maria Carmen taps on her laptop and narrows her eyes at the screen.

Brandon clears his throat. "They're from up north. They like to bury themselves in the snow."

Talib pats Brandon on the back. "Twenty points for the new guy."

Pointing to her laptop screen, Maria Carmen says, "There was a solar eclipse in Canada three years ago."

I add the information to the list in my sketchbook and ask, "What about the snake?"

"It looks like a boa constrictor," Brandon says. "Those are from Central and South America."

I look at him and smile. I'm impressed.

Maria Carmen stops typing on her keyboard. "And there was a solar eclipse in Panama nineteen years ago."

"My abuela said that the tule vieja story comes from Panama. Maybe that's the first animal she figured out she could turn into."

Maria Carmen takes my sketchbook and scans the page about the tule vieja. "It's good to know this information about her, but I think our priority should be getting Brandon's dad and your abuela back." Maria

Carmen turns to Brandon. "We know your dad was wrapped up in spider silk."

Brandon nods, and Maria Carmen reaches into the drawer of her nightstand. She pulls out a pocketknife with her brother's initials, CMC, engraved on the side. "So I think we're definitely going to need this to cut him out."

Brandon reaches into his jacket and pulls out his own pocketknife. Maria Carmen gives him a tight smile.

I take my sketchbook back from Maria Carmen and flip to a blank page. I scrawl *Brilliant Plan to Defeat the Tule Vieja* across the top. "First, we have to figure out where in the quarry the tule vieja is keeping Brandon's dad and my abuela," I say.

"Then we free them," Maria Carmen adds.

"And finally, we miraculously beat the tule vieja."

"Hopefully without getting bitten in the process," Talib says.

"All before the eclipse. Which is tomorrow."

"Sounds like a soup sandwich." Brandon chuckles.

I look at Brandon. I thought Dad and I were the only ones who talked about soup sandwiches.

"Excuse me, a what?" Maria Carmen asks.

"He means that it sounds impossible," I explain. "Like trying to eat a soup sandwich."

Talib throws his hands in the air. "Well, I've completely lost my appetite."

Later that night, while Maria Carmen is cocooned in her bed and Brandon snores on the floor, Talib grabs my sketchbook and flips through the pages of deer, coyote, and raven drawings. He stops when he gets to my Days in New Haven page.

"What's this?" he asks.

"I keep track of how many days I've lived in each of the places the Army has moved us."

Talib flips back and looks at the tick marks for Fort Hood, Fort Campbell, Fort Lewis, Fort Carson, and Fort Benning.

"You mark every single day?"

I sigh. "Yeah, it pretty much ends up being a countdown. We always move again."

Talib closes the sketchbook and slides it over to me. "Well, I hope you get to make a million marks for New Haven," he says, rolling over and shoving Maria Carmen's spare pillow under his head.

I turn onto my back and stare at the ceiling. Even with a vicious tule vieja roaming the woods and Abuela gone, I can't help but agree.

I've done the stupidest thing I've ever done in all our moves. I've let New Haven become home.

CHAPTER 23

I CAN'T SLEEP. I want to email Dad, but I know I can't. I don't even know what I could possibly say without completely destroying Mom's Always Be Positive, Always Be Happy rule. But I just want to talk to my dad.

I drag my backpack over to where I'm lying on Maria Carmen's floor. I rummage through it, trying to see if Talib packed me a hoodie, when I grab something unexpected: Dad's animal encyclopedia.

I flip through the pages, looking over Dad's drawings of hawks, wild hogs, and armadillos. A note scrawled next to the hog says, *Mami told me that hogs only like jokes in Spanish. They don't think English jokes are funny. At all.*

I run my hand over the page, smiling at the other notes: Armadillos dare one another to take on cars. Hummingbirds are actually scared of heights. Most bats really wish they were house cats.

I wish Abuela had told Dad how to defeat a tule vieja who could turn into a spider, a snake, and a wolverine. That would be good to find in the encyclopedia right now.

Thoughts of spiderwebs and wolverine claws swirl in my head until my eyelids become heavy. I'm about to doze off when I feel tight pressure on my chest.

My eyes slam open as I gasp for air. I see a large brown snake curling around my torso. Her head makes its way to my chest, and she flicks my chin with her tongue.

"Your family is gone," she hisses. "And here you are, my dear, with no home. You knew this would happen, didn't you?"

I'm about to pass out when the snake uncoils from my body and slithers to the window. She slides out into the night, her slick skin gleaming in the moonlight.

My eyes open again. I sit up and catch my breath.

It was just a dream.

The air still stings my lungs. Morning light streams through Maria Carmen's bedroom window, which is hanging open. I look over to her bed and find it empty. I'm the only one lying on the floor. Talib and Brandon are gone, too.

Did everyone wake up before me?

I slip my backpack over my shoulders and start to head downstairs.

"No! Let me go!"

I hear a shout outside and rush to the window. The wild-haired woman from last night is dragging Brandon to the edge of the woods. He struggles against her, but she twists his arms behind his back into submission, her long fingernails digging into his skin.

I cram my feet into my shoes and crawl out of Maria Carmen's window, sliding down the shingles and jumping to the ground. I race through the woods, following Brandon's shouts.

Suddenly, I'm hit in the stomach and fall to the ground. I try to suck in a breath and struggle to fill my lungs. The tule vieja stands above me, her eyes rimmed with red, her skin a mottled gray. Veins in her forearms pop as she grips a twisted oak branch.

I kick my legs out and smack her in the knee, making her double over and drop the large stick in her hands. I rush over to Brandon, lying on the ground, holding his arm.

"You okay?" I ask.

Brandon grunts. "Not the wake-up call I was looking for."

The tule vieja pounds her fists on the ground. A scream erupts from deep in her throat as fur sprouts from her body. I hear the bones in her fingers crack as long claws shoot from her fingernails.

Brandon grabs a large rock next to him and launches it at the tule vieja. "It's too early in the morning for this!" he groans.

The rock smacks the tule vieja between the eyes, then a small trickle of blood runs down her wolverine snout. She snarls and takes off toward the quarry. Her paws thud against the dirt as she disappears between the trees.

"Where are Talib and Maria Carmen?" I ask Brandon.

"I think she took them." His voice quivers.

My stomach turns over. I swallow hard.

I stand and help Brandon up. "I woke up when I felt a spider on my face," he says.

"Did she bite you?" I ask, my eyes searching Brandon for signs of a welt.

Brandon shakes his head. "Talib was right. A shoe works. Except she turned into a snake before I could get her. She wrapped around me and slid me out the window." Brandon hunches over, hands on his knees. "I don't think I've ever been so scared. We've got to get her, Nestor."

I stretch my back and catch my breath. "That's exactly what we're going to do," I tell him, hiking my backpack up on my shoulders. "Let's go."

We jog into the woods. I look up at the sky, the sun rising higher. Somewhere in the bright sky, the moon is starting its march toward the sun. I'm not sure how long we have until the eclipse. As we reach the edge of the woods, I look down at the dry creek between them and the quarry. The reality of what I'm about to face catches up with me. All I've got are the shoes on my feet and a sixth grader with questionable hunting skills next to me. That's all we've got against a shape-shifting witch.

Brandon and I slide down to the dry creek bed, dirt pouring into our shoes, and scramble up the other side. I jog to the edge of the quarry, but each step is a marathon. My joints crack at the slightest movement, and my muscles tremble.

Before us is an enormous pit carved out of lime-stone. Steep, pale cliffs with claw marks left by earth-moving machines lead down to a dirt floor. A single cave has been dug into the cliff straight in front of us, its black interior hiding whatever is inside. Large piles of rocks fill the quarry floor, creating a maze. Brandon groans next to me.

Mentally, I run through what we have to do. Find Abuela, Talib, Maria Carmen, and Brandon's dad. Stop the tule vieja. Avoid getting bitten by wolverines or snakes.

No problem.

"Nestor, wait," Brandon says next to me. His hand on my shoulder makes me jump.

"What?"

"I think the cavalry has arrived."

CHAPTER 24

I TURN AND SEE A SWARM OF ANIMALS behind us. Deer, coyote, ravens, squirrels. Even an armadillo and some foxes. Lumbering behind the crowd of animals is a large black bear.

"Let's do this. I'm so ready to poop on a witch!" Cuervito squawks, hopping up and down on the ground.

Chela walks forward and lowers her head toward me. "We're here to help, Nestor. Just tell us what to do."

I look at Brandon, and he shrugs. "Go ahead. Do your thing," he says.

We gather at the edge of the quarry cliff with our animal army. "Where do you think they are?" Val asks.

I bite my lip and think. "Well, if it were me, I'd hide everybody in that cave. So that's probably the first place we should check."

"On it," says Cuervito, taking off into the yellowing sky. An orange haze has settled in the air as the moon moves closer to the sun.

Brandon nudges my arm with his elbow. "We're gonna have to go down there, you know. We can use the piles of rocks for cover, but we have to make sure we maintain visibility with each other and signal when we've checked for safety."

I stare at Brandon, and he grins sheepishly. I think Dad would actually like him.

"Sounds good," I tell him. Reaching into my backpack, I pull out Dad's collapsible baton. With one swift flick of a wrist, it becomes a metal rod that could stop a charging wolverine. "Take this," I say, handing the baton to Brandon.

I pull out Dad's heavy-duty flashlight and grip it in my hand, the metal cold against my skin. "It'll be dark in the cave, so we'll need this."

Brandon looks at the sun and squints. The burnt orange sky has fooled the crickets into thinking dusk is coming, and their chirping fills the air. The eclipse is getting closer. "It's gonna be dark out here soon. We'd better hurry."

Cuervito returns and lands at my feet. "They're in the cave," he says.

"Any sign of the tule vieja?" I ask.

"No. But I got some white lightning brewing for her when she does show up."

I look at the animals around us. The black bear is pawing his huge claws in the dirt. The armadillo is rolled into a tight ball, the two foxes pushing him around. The squirrels are shoving acorns into their cheeks and spitting them at Chela. Without these animals, it would just be me and Brandon. And if I couldn't understand them, we'd be lost.

Maybe our chances aren't so bad after all.

"All right. Let's do this," I tell them.

We circle the edge of the quarry and find a sloping hill that leads to the bottom. Brandon and I slide down on our backsides as the animals scamper over the rocks. We jog toward the cave dug into the side of the quarry cliff. Its gaping entry turns darker as the moon begins to cover the edge of the sun.

Brandon tugs at my arm as we approach the cave. "When we get in there, make sure you—"

A black blur slams into Brandon and throws him several feet away to the base of a huge pile of rocks.

"Brandon!"

I run over to him. The wolverine backs away from Brandon, scuffing her claws on the ground and blowing hot air through her nostrils.

Brandon eases himself off the ground, shakes his head, and brushes his hands on his jeans.

"You okay?" I ask.

"Yeah. It'll take more than a rabid rodent to knock me out," he says, clenching his fists.

The wolverine lowers her head, ready to charge again. "You shouldn't have come," she says.

The tule vieja charges again. I dodge to the right, and Brandon climbs up the rock pile out of the way. The wolverine slams into the rocks, tumbling several down on top of herself. She heaves her body out from under them and shakes her head.

The wolverine turns and glares at me with large black eyes. "You're more trouble than you're worth."

The black bear runs up behind me. "We've got this, Nestor. We can hold her off. Go get your people."

The wolverine charges again, and the black bear lowers his head, his thick arms and large claws ready to wrap around the incoming mass of teeth and fur. Brandon jumps down from the rock pile, and we race toward the cave. I hear a scream behind me and glance back to see black fur flying as the tule vieja morphs into a snake.

We run into the cave and stop, pressing our backs to the cave wall. I wait for my eyes to adjust to the darkness. What little light seeps inside the mouth of the cave doesn't do much to help me see inside.

"Dude, your flashlight," Brandon whispers next to me.

I lower my head. "Yeah, uh, I dropped it out there."

"Seriously?"

I feel something brush my leg, and I jump.

"You fellas need some night vision?" I look down and see Val at my feet.

"Yes, we do."

"All right. Follow me," he says, trotting farther into the cave.

I nudge Brandon. "The coyote will be our guide."

He chuckles. "Dude, I know we're on a rescue mission trying not to get attacked by a witch . . . but this is the coolest thing that's ever happened to me."

Brandon and I follow Val down a passageway. Squinting in the dark, I see sparkling mounds of white on the ground. I run closer and find two spider-silk cocoons, each containing a person shivering inside.

I race toward the first cocoon, which has light purple hair sprouting from the top.

"Buela!"

I try to pry the spider silk off her. It's wrapped tightly around her body and almost cuts through my skin when I pull on it. This isn't like any regular spiderweb I've ever seen.

Brandon crouches down next to Abuela. "Dad!" he says. He paws at the spider silk, but he can't get it off, either.

"Use your knife," I tell him.

He feels the pockets of his jacket, then lets loose a word that Abuela would give me a smack on the back of the head for if I ever said it.

"I think I left it at Maria Carmen's."

Val huffs behind us. "You two are an expert rescue team. I tell you what, I'll be right back."

He scampers down the passageway toward the entrance of the cave.

"Val's getting help," I tell Brandon.

I put my hand on top of Abuela's head. She squirms in the cocoon. "Niño?" she mumbles.

"I'm here, Abuela. I'm here. We're gonna get you out."

Val returns, a bobcat by his side.

"You know, for two animal-trivia geniuses," he scoffs, "I'm surprised you didn't know bobcats have incredibly sharp claws."

"Perfect!" Brandon looks at me. "You know, bobcats have really sharp claws."

The bobcat tilts his head at Brandon. "That's what I said. Name's Rufus, by the way. Your savior, Rufus."

Rufus lifts a thick paw and makes quick work of the cocoon around Abuela, slashing through the tightly bound silk. Abuela tumbles into my arms with a sigh.

"Are you okay?" I ask, my voice breaking.

"Sí, mi niño. I've been through worse than this," Abuela says, a soft chuckle rising from her throat.

Rufus moves over to Brandon's dad, slashing through the silk and freeing him from the cocoon. Brandon grabs his dad's arms to steady him.

"There's my boy," Brandon's dad says. He pulls Brandon into a hug, and I watch them, swallowing down the lump in my throat.

Brandon's dad looks from his son to Val and the bobcat. "I'm sure you have a good explanation for all this, son, but I'll wait to hear it," he says, groaning and stretching his arms.

Brandon gives his dad another hug. "Good. Because I'll need to figure out what the heck I'm going to say."

Abuela leans on me. "We need to get your friends."

I turn to Val. "There are two more cocoons here. We need to find them."

Brandon's dad whispers in his son's ear, "Did he just—"

Brandon holds up his finger to his mouth. "Later. It'll all make sense later. Maybe."

I hear him scamper farther into the cave. After a minute, he shouts, "They're here! They're here!"

"Go! Get them!" I say to Rufus. He takes off running down the cave.

Our heavy breathing echoes through the cave as Abuela, Brandon, his dad, and I wait for Val and Rufus to return with Maria Carmen and Talib.

We hear shuffling coming from deeper in the cave. Abuela grabs my hand as the sound grows closer.

And then I hear a voice. "I'm going to snap that snake's neck into a thousand pieces."

Maria Carmen.

"We're here, guys!" I call. "Just follow the bobcat."

The steps quicken, and soon Maria Carmen and Talib stand in front of us. Maria Carmen wraps her arms around me, and Talib slaps me on the back.

"Ay, mis niños," Abuela says, taking us all in her arms.

"Thanks for coming to get us," Maria Carmen says. She looks sheepishly at Brandon and mumbles, "Thanks."

Rufus nudges my shin with his head. "There are a lot more animals down there," he says, indicating the dark cave with his paw. "We should get them out, too."

I translate Rufus's message for everyone, and Brandon and I take off farther down the passageway with Rufus. Maria Carmen and Talib stay with Brandon's dad and Abuela as Maria Carmen continues to curse the tule vieja.

Brandon and I stop in front of row upon row of shiny spider-silk cocoons. Rufus licks his paw and says, "Give the professional some room to work, please."

I pull Brandon back as Rufus slashes at each of the cocoons, revealing dogs, cats, rabbits, and goats. He takes longer on an incredibly large cocoon that reveals a brown horse when the spider silk falls away. The horse shakes his black mane and asks for a carrot.

Brandon and I shoo the animals up the passageway as Rufus releases more and more. It looks like a zoo jailbreak flooding out of the cave.

Finally, we run back to Maria Carmen, Talib, Abuela, and Brandon's dad. "Let's get out of here," I tell them.

"Follow me!" Val shouts.

"You heard him. Let's go!" I say, starting to run out of the cave.

"Nestor, we don't speak coyote," Talib mumbles, following me with the others into the darkening quarry.

CHAPTER 25

BURSTING FROM THE CAVE, we see the eclipse is almost in full effect. The moon stretches across half the sun, casting long shadows throughout the quarry.

"We have to find the tule vieja," I tell Abuela. "She'll be even more powerful after the eclipse is over. Then we'll never be able to stop her."

"Of course, mi niño," Abuela says, still unable to catch her breath. She's in no condition to fight a witch.

I turn to Brandon's dad. "Mister . . . um, Brandon's

dad. Do you think you could take care of my abuela? I don't think she's up for a fight."

Brandon's dad reaches out to Abuela, and she takes his arm. I notice a tattoo below the crook of his elbow reading USMC.

"I know she'll be in good hands with a Marine," I tell him. Brandon's dad lowers his head and smiles.

"You sure you kids got this?" Brandon's dad asks. He stretches his back and winces, rubbing an old scar at the base of his neck. "You don't need any help from a worn-out Marine?"

I shake my head. "We can do it, sir. But my abuela really needs someone with her right now."

Brandon's dad straightens his shoulders. "I'll get her home. Don't worry. And you kids be careful. That witch is one mean lady."

"Dale un chancletazo para mi, niño," Abuela says, letting Brandon's dad lead her up and out of the quarry. "Chao, pescao."

"Y a la vuelta, picadillo," I call after her.

Maria Carmen, Talib, Brandon, and I crouch behind a pile of rocks on the quarry floor. The bear that was holding off the tule vieja is nowhere in sight.

"Are you really going to smack the tule vieja with

a sandal, like your abuela said?" Maria Carmen asks, chuckling.

"Nah," I tell her. "I left my smacking sandals at home."

A squirrel runs up to us, panting and scratching at the ground. "We've got her cornered up at the edge of the quarry. Hurry."

Maria Carmen, Talib, and Brandon look at me, waiting for a squirrel translation. "She's up there," I say, pointing above us to the woods.

"Let's get this over with," Talib says, pushing himself up from behind the rocks.

Brandon grabs his arm. "Wait. We shouldn't all come at her from the same direction. We should, um . . . What's the word, Nestor?"

"Flank her?"

"Yep, that's it. Flank her."

"Good plan," I tell him. "Talib, you and Brandon go through the woods and come at the tule vieja from behind. Maria Carmen and I will come at her from here, right up out of the quarry."

"I'll show them the way," the squirrel says.

I point to our furry friend and tell Talib and Brandon, "Just follow the squirrel."

Talib shakes his head. "Just when you think it couldn't get any weirder."

Brandon and Talib take off after the squirrel while Maria Carmen and I make our way across the quarry floor to the slope where we entered. I'm almost to the last pile of rocks when I'm knocked off my feet. I slam into the dirt, the breath sucked out of my lungs.

I hear Maria Carmen shout, "Get away from him!"

I look up and see Miss Humala.

"Just wait, Nestor," she says. "A little bit longer and the eclipse will be complete. She'll get what she wants and leave. She's already furious that you kept her from taking more animals. Just let her have a few more."

I look past her into the sky. The moon has almost completely covered the sun.

"I'm not letting her hurt anyone else," I say. I stand, my back aching and my hands bloodied from the gravel. I brush my palms on my jeans. "We have to stop her, and you know it."

Miss Humala charges at me again. Maria Carmen yanks my arm and pulls me out of the way. We scramble up the rock pile away from Miss Humala.

"I know she's your mother," Maria Carmen says, "but you can't just let her do this!"

Miss Humala pounds her fists into the rocks. "I've been trying to stop her for years! I thought I could run away from her, but it was no use."

"But we can help you," I tell her. "We can stop her together."

Miss Humala shakes her head. "You're fools. She's been doing this my whole life. Do you know what it's like being dragged everywhere across the globe while your mother chases eclipses? She's growing more and more powerful. She'll never stop." Her head snaps up at us, her eyes black and darting in every direction. "But I can stop *you*."

Her arms flail, and she starts to climb up the rock pile toward us.

"No!" I shout, launching myself at Miss Humala and knocking us both off the rock pile. I feel a snap beneath me as I land on her arm and we crash to the ground.

Maria Carmen slides down the rock pile behind me. "Miss Humala, stop," she pleads.

"We can help you stop her," I say, getting up and holding my hands out to her.

Miss Humala stands, holding an arm that hangs at an unnatural angle. Her shoulders shudder as she sighs. "She . . . she'll grow weak if . . ." Miss Humala stops and presses her lips together.

"If what?" Maria Carmen says. "Tell us!"

Miss Humala shakes her head as tears fall from her cheeks. "If she gains power from biting an animal, the opposite holds true as well."

I hear a scream echo off the quarry walls. It sounds a lot like Talib.

Maria Carmen and I run from Miss Humala. I see her scramble up the quarry wall and disappear into the woods. Climbing to the edge of the quarry, Maria Carmen and I peek into the woods.

Maria Carmen gasps and covers her mouth. Talib and Brandon lie on the ground, eyes closed, large red welts burning their necks. Rufus is wrapped in a spider-silk cocoon, unconscious.

"The eclipse is upon us," the tule vieja says, seething. "Just one bite and I will have your power."

I look up at the sky. The sun still casts a thin, slivered crescent from behind the moon.

The tule vieja takes a long, bony finger and drags it along the side of the spider cocoon, exposing Rufus's torso. Long fangs grow from her teeth, glistening in what light the sun still radiates. She snaps her head back and plunges her fangs into his body. He shudders and squirms under the tight silk threads.

Withdrawing from her prey, the tule vieja wipes her mouth with the back of her hand, her fangs retracting into her gums. Her body begins to shudder as spotted golden fur sprouts from her skin. The bones in her hands crack as they form paws with sharp claws on the end and her ears twitch into furry black points.

"That isn't good," Maria Carmen whispers next to me.

Just as quickly as they sprouted, though, the tule vieja's claws push back into her hands as her ears round out and fur falls from her body. She's human again.

The sun is still peeking out in the smallest sliver from behind the moon. The tule vieja is too early.

"No!" she cries, her voice echoing off the quarry walls.

I reach for a rock near me and throw it straight at her; it thuds against the back of her head. She stumbles forward and spins around to face me as I crawl over the edge of the quarry. The whites of her eyes are completely bloodred, her skin a scaly gray.

Her shoulders heave as she catches her breath. Her

eyes narrow at me, and a sick smile grows from the corners of her mouth. "My dear, I don't think you realize the gift you've given me," she says. "Why would I want a bobcat's power . . . when I can have yours?"

I swallow hard. "Then let him go. You don't need him," I shout, hoping the shaking in my voice doesn't betray my fear.

She moves slowly toward me. "So eager to sacrifice yourself for them," she says, waving a bony hand at Talib and Brandon, lying on the ground. Behind them lie a squirrel, the armadillo, and a fox, all wrapped in cocoons and paralyzed by spider bites.

I grab a larger rock and clench it in my fist. "Let them all go."

The smile on the tule vieja's face exposes yellow jagged teeth, and a sinister chuckle rises from her throat. "Imagine if I could do what you can do. Talk to them all. Understand them. They'd be powerless against me."

The tule vieja paces in front of the injured Rufus, closing the distance between us. My fist closes tightly on the rock in my hand. She inches toward me, and I launch the rock at her. She winces as it hits her thigh but keeps advancing.

I spot Maria Carmen out of the corner of my eye, crawling up out of the quarry and inching toward the bobcat behind the tule vieja's back.

The tule vieja clicks her tongue. She looks up at the sky. The moon has completely covered the sun. An electric ring bursts around the shadow of the moon. I have six minutes until the total eclipse passes.

I think about what Miss Humala said. If the tule vieja gets power from biting animals, then the opposite is true. Does that mean she will lose her powers if animals bite her?

"It's time!" the tule vieja cries. She rushes at me.

"No!" I throw my body at her, knocking her to the ground. She pushes me off her, digging her fingers into my shoulders.

I stand between my friends and the tule vieja. "You're not hurting any of us."

The tule vieja purses her lips. She looks up at the eclipse, still in full formation. Her red eyes flash, and she lunges at me. Pinning me to the ground, she blows her hot breath in my face.

I groan and struggle against the tule vieja. "Just don't hurt them. If you let my friends go, I'll let you bite me," I manage to say, hoping that a rhinoceros will charge out of the woods and demolish the tule vieja so I don't have to keep my end of the bargain.

Crouching down, the tule vieja whispers in my ear, "Who says I won't just take your little friends when I'm done with you, anyway?"

I squirm underneath her as her front teeth grow into snake fangs. My body begins to tremble and shake. I can hear my heartbeat thudding in my ears.

"Stop moving, my dear," the tule vieja says as she strains against me. "I'll make this quick."

I snap my head toward the woods, searching for some sign of the animals who helped us earlier. Brandon and Talib are still on the ground, paralyzed by the tule vieja's spider bite. Maria Carmen is trying to free Rufus but can't cut through the spider silk, her hands red from trying.

I look up at the sky and see Cuervito soaring above us.

"Oh man, oh man, oh man," he exclaims, circling the eclipse.

"Get help!" I choke out.

The tule vieja leans in close to my neck. I feel the sharp point of her fangs press against my skin. I squeeze my eyes shut, waiting for her bite, helpless to stop it.

I hear hoofbeats to my right, and the tule vieja is thrown off me in a blur of fangs and antlers. I roll over and crouch on the ground. A large buck stands between the tule vieja and me, hooves scratching in the dirt, antlers lowered. The tule vieja is crumpled on the ground, pawing at the rocks around her.

The total eclipse is starting to break.

"No! I need you. I can't waste this time. This is my last chance!"

She slams her fist on the ground and scrambles toward the buck. The coyote bursts out of the woods and lunges at the tule vieja's face, scratching her along her cheek. A burst of orange flames erupts along the lines of the cuts.

I run over to Maria Carmen and the bobcat, my hands still shaking.

A scream rips through the air. The tule vieja is lying on the ground, her long fingers clawing into the dirt as her body shudders. The scales on her skin are growing thick and brown. Her body grows longer and longer. With one final scream, she transforms into a snake.

"Run!" the buck shouts to us.

The tule vieja hisses and slithers toward Talib and Brandon. Cuervito flies at her and sinks his talons right behind her thick head. Val stands in front of Talib and Brandon and growls at the tule vieja. He turns and licks the spider bites on their necks. They begin to stir.

Chela runs over to Talib and Brandon, helping them up with a nudge of her head. "Get them home," I tell her. They lean on her torso, still shaking their heads from the effects of the spider venom, and stumble off into the woods.

"We need to finish this, Nestor," the buck tells me.

Val has the tule vieja pinned to the ground with his paws. She snaps her fangs inches from his nose, spewing his face with spit. He sinks his teeth into her neck. Another fiery burst shoots from the puncture wound, and the tule vieja's eyes grow rounder, turning from snake to wolverine.

"That's it," I say. "She gets weaker every time she's bitten!"

The tule vieja whips her tail around the coyote's torso and squeezes, forcing him to release her. Val backs away from the tule vieja and growls, baring his teeth and lunging at the snake, but she slams her thick tail into his body, sending him flying into a large tree.

The tule vieja rockets toward me and the buck. I pick up a large stick and smash it across her face. She whips her tail and wraps it around my body, crushing my arms so I can't move.

"Bite!" I cry, hoping the animals nearby will hear me. "You have to bite!"

The snake lifts her head and stares her wolverine eyes into mine. "Oh, I plan to, my dear. I plan to."

The tule vieja looks up and sees the moon beginning to move past the sun again, breaking the corona. "There's no more time," she hisses. "I've always wanted to be able to talk to my prey."

Her long fangs draw closer to my face as her jaw grows wider and wider. It looks like she's going to swallow me whole. I look past the tule vieja's gaping mouth and see the buck stomp down on her tail with his hoof, forcing the tule vieja to release her hold on me. The buck lowers his head, scooping up the tule vieja in his antlers, and with a sharp flick of his neck, he sends her flying into the woods.

"I'm getting tired of this witch," he says.

"You and me both," I mutter, sucking in a breath.

"We have to get everyone we can to bite her. That's the only way to take away her power."

"You got it. You got it," a squirrel says, scampering to my side. "I'll spread the word. Let everyone know."

We hear a scream erupt from the woods, and the tule vieja's snake form bursts from the trees. She rockets toward me, and I roll to the side to avoid her exposed fangs. The buck plunges his antlers into the ground around her, trapping the flailing snake.

Cuervito soars down from the sky and pecks the tule vieja's back. Small flames shoot out of her scales, and tufts of black fur shoot up in their place.

The tule vieja squirms and hisses as Val approaches, his small, sharp teeth bared. He bites into her side over and over, sending bright sparks into the air. Furry legs sprout from her body as she continues to push against the buck's antlers.

Val lunges at the tule vieja, growling, and sinks his teeth just behind her head. Her round snout turns pointed as whiskers grow from her scales and furry ears push from her head.

Kicking her legs, the snake, now almost completely transformed into a wolverine, pushes against the buck's antlers and frees herself from the ground.

She snarls at the animals circling her, looking for an opportunity to bite.

Maria Carmen and I hear huffs coming from the woods, and a large black form emerges from the trees.

"You have to bite her! Go. Go!" Maria Carmen shouts at the bear.

The massive bear lumbers toward the tule vieja, covered in scales and fur, and wraps his arms around her. He sinks his teeth into her neck. A burst of light fills the quarry edge, and I squint my eyes shut.

A scream rips through the air as the bear pushes the tule vieja to the edge of the cliff, her feet clawing frantically in the dirt. Releasing his bite from her neck, the bear slams his paws into the tule vieja's chest. She falls down the edge of the quarry, flailing as she drops. Her body smacks hard on a jagged rock on the quarry floor, and a snap echoes through the air.

Maria Carmen and I run to the cliff's edge and look down. The tule vieja's body lies at unnatural angles between two large boulders. We hold our breath, waiting for some sign of movement from the tangled mass of fur and claws. But none comes.

She's gone.

"She didn't turn human," Maria Carmen says. "She

kept growing weaker, but she never turned back into a human."

"Maybe she never *was* human," I say, shuddering at the thought.

The quarry fills with light as the sun breaks out from behind the moon. The eclipse is over. The shadow of the tule vieja's body stretches along the rocks as the increasing sunlight sharpens her shadow into spiderwebs stretching through the quarry.

CHAPTER 26

Dear Dad,

So it turns out New Haven isn't as boring
as I thought it would be. Go figure.

We have a new trivia club sponsor,
Coach Rodriguez. Our old sponsor, Miss
Humala, decided to take a long vacation
far away from New Haven. I guess teaching
photosynthesis and the phases of the moon
to snotty sixth graders became too much.
Coach Rodriguez isn't bad. He sometimes
forgets he's talking to kids about animal
trivia and not coaching the football team,

so he blows the loud whistle around his neck when we get a question wrong. Before our last competition, he told us to "leave it all out on the field."

I'm not sure what we're supposed to do with that.

Brandon's actually ended up being a good member of our team. Did I tell you his dad was in the Marine Corps? He was never deployed, though. He hurt his back during a training exercise and was honorably discharged. Brandon says his dad really misses being a Marine. Do you think you'd miss being in the Army?

Did Mom tell you about all the craziness out at the quarry? They found a dead wolverine on the rocks. Now everybody's saying it's too dangerous to go in the woods, just in case there are other wolverines out there.

But I think we'll be okay.

And did you see the eclipse? I don't think it was visible in Afghanistan. It was pretty interesting here, though. Did you know that some people believe you can get special powers during an eclipse? That would be crazy, right? You could learn to fly or gain super-strength.

Maybe you could even talk to animals.

Love you. Stay safe.
Nestor

"Hey, put your sketchbook down," Talib says, nudging my elbow. "We need a judge."

Brandon drags a plate piled high with Flamin' Hot Cheetos across the picnic table in Abuela's backyard. "We're gonna see who can fit more Cheetos in their mouth."

I shake my head. "Nope. I'm no judge—I'm the champion," I tell them, grabbing a handful of Cheetos and shoving them into my mouth.

Talib and Brandon look at each other and grab Cheetos, stuffing them into their mouths.

"Gentlemen, I'm fairly certain that's an easy way to choke," my mom says, clearing her throat behind us.

"But we'll die winners," I mumble through Cheetos, spewing crumbs across the table.

"You'll die idiots," Maria Carmen says, sitting down next to Brandon, a hamburger and chips on her plate.

Brandon's dad is manning the grill on Abuela's porch as Ms. Cordova and Talib's mom lay out salads on the table. We're having a barbecue to celebrate the trivia team's latest win. Our triumph over San Jermin Middle School has kept our undefeated streak intact.

After we left the tule vieja at the quarry, the animals in town stopped disappearing. Dogs, cats, goats, horses, and even a stray hamster managed to find their way back to their owners. Talib's dog, George, herded Maria Carmen's lost goats right up to Talib's backyard and tried to let them all in the house through the doggie door. And since Abuela doesn't need to tromp through the woods anymore, people eventually forgot that they were mad at her and moved on to the next thing, like the fact that New Haven High School won its first basketball game in five years.

"You know what we should've done to Coach Rodriguez after our win?" Talib asks, stealing a potato chip off Maria Carmen's plate.

She smacks his hand. "What?"

"Dumped a cooler of Gatorade over his head."

Brandon laughs, almost choking on a Cheeto.

Mom slaps his back. "I told you," she says, raising an eyebrow. She goes back inside the house to help Abuela with dessert.

Brandon's dad sets a plate of hamburgers down between us. "Chow time, boys. And lady," he adds, winking at Maria Carmen. "You need your strength for your next competition."

He pauses and puts his hand on Brandon's shoulder. "And for anything else that might come up, right?"

Talib and I nod. Brandon's dad never flat-out talked about what happened in the woods with the tule vieja. But the next week at school, Brandon slid a pin across the cafeteria table. It was the globe and anchor that all Marines wear on their dress uniforms.

"My dad wanted you to have this," he said.

I examined the pin, its gold surface shining under the cafeteria lights. I took it and put it on my backpack, right under the LOPEZ name tape Dad always has sewn to his uniform. The Army and Marine Corps, together. I chuckled at what Dad would think.

Maria Carmen and Talib get up with their plates and head over to the picnic table Abuela has piled high with food. Brandon and I sit, watching Cuervito hop closer and closer to the plate Talib's mom is ignoring.

"You know, what you can do is pretty cool," Brandon says so softly I barely hear him.

"Thanks," I mutter, pushing a chip around on my plate with a half-eaten hamburger. I look over at Brandon's dad, flipping more burgers on the grill. "I'm glad your dad's okay."

Brandon swallows a large bite of burger and nods. He whispers, "Yours too."

I nod, swallowing the lump in my throat.

Maria Carmen and Talib return, arguing about whose mom makes better mac and cheese.

I shake my head and get up to fill my plate with Abuela's empanadas.

"Hey there, champion," Mom says, picking the sesame seeds off her hamburger bun as she sits on the steps of the patio.

I sit down next to her as she brushes discarded seeds off her lap.

"I noticed something in your room today," she says.

My mind races through what could possibly be in there. Did Val make himself at home again? Did she find the Texas history quiz I failed?

"Um, you did?" I ask, pulling on the hem of my shirt.

"You unpacked everything!" she says, nudging me.

I smile, stealing a chip off her plate. "Yeah. It's not so bad here at Abuela's."

"Not so bad?" Mom says, pointing to the picnic table where Maria Carmen and Talib are trying to see who can throw sliced pickles into Brandon's mouth. "I'd say it's pretty good."

I laugh. "Yeah. It is pretty good. I'll admit it."

Mom sighs and sets her plate down next to her. She grabs my hand and squeezes. "It would be better with your dad here, wouldn't it?"

I put my head on her shoulder. "Everything would be better with Dad here."

We watch Cuervito peck at the hamburger Talib's mom abandoned as Abuela brings out Ms. Cordova's churros, setting them on the picnic table where my friends sit. Laughter floats through the air and fills our lungs.

I trace the lines on Mom's hand with my thumb, a map of all the places we've been. All the new schools, new houses, new people. Her hand has always been there, holding mine.

"Thanks, Mom," I tell her.

She looks at me. "Thanks for what?"

"For everything." I shrug. "For making sure my friends don't choke on chips. For letting Abuela make me pastelitos for breakfast. And lunch. And dinner. For making us come to New Haven."

"Oh, lordy, I wish I could've recorded that! Your father will never believe me otherwise."

I shake my head. "You're never going to let me live that down, are you?"

Mom laughs. "I'm having it printed in your yearbook senior year. Guaranteed!"

Mom pushes me up off the steps, and I head back over to the picnic table. I sit back down next to Talib.

"Brandon says you can smack him," Talib says through a mouthful of churros.

"And why would I do that?"

"He spilled ketchup on your sketchbook."

Brandon slides my sketchbook across the table. "Sorry, man. It squirted out like a horse fart."

I flip through the pages and stop at a drawing I made of a wolverine. A large red streak is smeared across the page.

Maria Carmen leans across the table and looks at the drawing. "That actually looks more accurate."

I nod. "Yeah, I'm pretty sure Brandon improved it."

I flip through my sketchbook, looking at the drawings I've done. Cuervito pecking at Abuela's tomatoes. Val as he hid in my room. Chela eating breakfast in the woods. I even have a sketch of Talib's smile as he sits in science class. And Maria Carmen holding our trivia cards.

"What's that page?" Brandon asks as I flip to my Days in New Haven chart.

"Oh, I keep track of how many days I've spent in all the places I've lived. Usually, I eventually have to start a new page for somewhere else."

Maria Carmen scans the page. "There are only twenty-two marks on that page. You've been here longer than that."

I run my fingers across the page. "Yeah, I guess I've forgotten to make the marks each day. That was bound to happen with a crazy tule vieja terrorizing the town."

Talib raises an eyebrow. "I figured it was because you were just enjoying our company so much."

I smile and look at the faces around me at the table, hearing Abuela's laughter mix with Mom's.

Talib's right.

I close the notebook, running my hand over the

well-worn cover. Maybe I'll leave those pages blank, letting the days happen without counting down. Packing and unpacking boxes. Letting Dad come and go and come back again.

Most likely, I'll fill the pages, not with tick marks but with drawings of Talib as he tries to balance a pencil on his nose. Of Maria Carmen sticking her tongue out at her axolotl as he begs for more food. Of Brandon smearing his dad's camouflage paint across his face and hiding behind a mesquite bush. Of Abuela running her hand across new fabric at her sewing machine. Of Mom's knuckles as she pulls at the bottom of her scrubs.

I'll fill my notebook with drawings of home.

AUTHOR'S NOTE

The legend of the tule vieja originates from Panama and Costa Rica, two countries I lived in when I was younger. The bruja that terrorizes New Haven is a bit different from the traditional tule vieja. While the tule vieja that Nestor encounters can turn into various animals by biting them, the Panamanian and Costa Rican tule vieja takes on a permanent half-woman, half-bird form. Short batwings sprout from her back, and sharp hawk talons take the place of her feet. Wandering through towns at night, she searches for her lost children, drawn by the cries of newly born babies and the howls of dogs. Much like the Latin American tale of La Llorona, a woman who drowned her children and now searches for them along the riverbank, the tule vieja snatches small children from their homes, believing they are her own. As with most boogeyman tales, parents use the legend of the tule vieja to frighten their children away from wandering alone.

ACKNOWLEDGMENTS

I show love and appreciation through baking, so I owe a large plate of guava pastelitos to several people who helped bring this book into the world.

To my agent, Stefanie Sanchez Von Borstel, for seeing the potential in my story and pushing me to make it the best I could. I'm grateful for your enthusiasm, hard work, and, most of all, your friendship. I'm so excited to be a part of the Full Circle Literary family.

To my editor, Trisha de Guzman, for your patience and encouragement of me as a debut author. I'm grateful that you saw the heart of my story. You are incredible, and I'm thankful to work with you. To the entire team at Farrar Straus Giroux BYR/Macmillan, for your tireless work on my behalf and your boundless enthusiasm.

Several groups that support me daily need to hold a large potluck so we can celebrate. I'll bring the tostones and croquetas. To SCBWI Austin, I'm eternally in debt for the conference that introduced me to my wonderful agent. Thank you for your constant support of authors. To my Pitch Wars class of 2017, thank you for showing me how truly amazing the writing community is. To Las Musas and my Kidlit Latinx hermanas, thank you for proving that our stories matter and that our kids can be heroes.

To my phenomenal critique partner, Sarah Kapit, who read the earliest version of this story and encouraged me to keep writing when I was still nervous about claiming the title "author." To my Pitch Wars mentor, Jessica Bayliss, for pushing me to dig deeper and walking me through the revision process.

To Kimberly Zook, who read the opening chapters of this book and gave me the seal of approval as a military mom and wife. Military moms and dads have my highest admiration and gratitude for your ability to provide stability and love in ever-changing environments. This book is for you.

To my family: Mom, Dad, Heather, and Rob. Thank you for the love of stories you instilled in me. Thank you for tolerating my overactive and odd imagination growing up. Thank you for filling me with love, support, and happiness. Y para mis antepasados: Cumba y Abuela, Papa and Grandma Ethel, Grandma Grace, Tías Cuca y Gladys, y Tío Pineda: May your memory live on through my stories.

To my husband, Joe, who let me ask him a million questions, who celebrated my achievements, who came home. Love you.

And finally to my son, Soren. You are my inspiration. You are my joy. All my stories are for you.

Based on the author's family history,
a twelve-year-old boy leaves his family in
Cuba to immigrate to the US by himself . . .

Keep reading for an excerpt

CHAPTER 1

Santa Clara, Cuba
April 1961

This is not my home.

Tía Carmen's kitchen doesn't have my model of a P-51 Mustang or scattered pieces of Erector set. Instead of a mango tree out front with a tocororo nest in its branches, there's a crowd of soldiers, slapping one another on the back and firing their rifles into the night air.

My cousin Manuelito slaps another domino down on the table. "Doble ocho, tonto," he cackles. His stubby fingers fidget over the remaining dominoes in front of him.

"Don't call me stupid," I say, narrowing my eyes.

Mami paces behind Manuelito, twisting a red dish towel in her hands. She reaches for the cross at her neck, and I hear her mumble the Lord's Prayer. "Padre nuestro, que está en el cielo."

Sharp shouts outside Tía Carmen's house cut off the rest of her prayer.

"Mami?"

My little brother, Pepito, starts to get up from his chair, but Mami puts her hand on his shoulder.

"Don't worry, nene. It's fine."

Mami and Tía Carmen exchange worried looks. They may be fooling Pepito, but they're not fooling me. Fidel's soldiers defeated a force of Cuban refugees who had fled to the United States and were trained by the American government. The refugees tried to invade Cuba at the Bay of Pigs, but Fidel's army quickly overtook them. From what Papi told me, this was our last hope of ridding our island of Fidel's oppressive government.

"Keep playing, Cumba," Mami says as she waves her hand at me. The candle on the table where Manuelito and I sit flickers, bouncing long shadows of dominoes across the plastic floral tablecloth.

I try to focus on the tile in my hand, but the shouting outside increases. I shake my head and slap another domino down on the table. "Tranque. I blocked you."

The waistband of my pants digs into my stomach, and I fidget in my folding chair. The chair squeaks, prompting Mami to give me a quick look from the window.

She dries the same bowl over and over until the dish towel is limp in her hands. Tía Carmen tries to turn the radio up, but Mami snaps the volume dial down.

"I don't want to listen to that foolishness," she mutters.

Manuelito looks at me from across the table. The light from the candle turns his eyebrows into thick brown triangles, and his fat cheeks cast a shadow on his neck.

"Your papi come home yet?" He sneers, and the candlelight elongates his front teeth into fangs.

Tía Carmen crosses the kitchen in a blur of blue cotton flowers. She slaps Manuelito on the back of the head, his neck snapping forward and flipping his brown hair into his eyes.

"Cállate, niño," she hisses.

Manuelito's being told to shut up offers little consolation. He doesn't know. He has no idea that at this moment, my papi is tucked in a corner of our house, hiding from Fidel's soldiers. He sent us to Tía Carmen's when Radio Rebelde blasted the news of the impending Yanqui invasion.

"I don't want you here if they come for me," he

said as he ruffled my hair, the smile on his lips failing to hide the nervousness in his eyes. Fidel's soldiers were rounding up anyone who had worked for former President Batista. Papi was a captain in the army. Even though he was just a lawyer in the Judge Advocate General's unit, those two bars on his uniform made him look important.

I wrap my feet around the legs of the folding chair to keep myself from kicking Manuelito. He's a year younger than I am, and he prides himself on being the most annoying eleven-year-old in the world.

Manuelito lowers his head closer to the table, his eyebrows thickening and his fangs growing longer. He whispers, "It's not gonna work, you know. Fidel always wins."

I unwrap my left foot from the chair and kick him in the shin. Manuelito winces. That was for Papi.

Tía Carmen turns up the radio by the sink, and Mami purses her lips. "¡Aquí, Radio Rebelde!" shouts a deep voice from the speaker. "The Yanqui imperialists have failed, are failing, and will fail to overthrow our glorious revolution!"

News of the Bay of Pigs invasion fills the kitchen. Fidel has been giving speech after speech, taunting the Cuban exiles and their American supporters.

The anthem of the 26th of July Movement, Fidel's government, blasts from the radio, and Mami turns it off.

I sigh. Manuelito, Pepito, and I try to concentrate on our domino game. But it's no use. You're supposed to play with four people. Normally, Papi would've been our fourth.

Pepito lays down a new domino, and his eyes grow wide. "¡Ay, caramba! ¡La caja de muertos!"

He slaps his hand over his mouth before Mami can hear him curse. Pepito has always thought the double-nine tile was bad luck because it's called the dead man's box. When I hear the stomps and shouts outside, I'm reminded that there are worse sources of bad luck than a little white tile.

"It's okay, hermanito. Don't worry," I reassure him.

I swipe my hand over the dominoes we've laid down, erasing our careful rows. Game over. I show Pepito how to line up the dominoes in front of one another and knock them down in a cascade. He claps his chubby hands and starts to set up the dominoes himself, sticking out his tongue in concentration.

Mami sets down a glass of water in front of me, and I pretend not to notice her shaking hand. A sharp pop of gunfire explodes outside, making us all jump.

"What are they doing?" Pepito asks.

Mami lets out a long sigh. "They're celebrating, nene."

Pepito scrunches up his face. "That doesn't sound like celebrating to me. There isn't any music."

Eventually they will have music. Of course they will have music. And parades. And speeches. So many speeches. That's what they always do.

But there are always guns first.

More pops of gunfire burst outside. We hear a whizz and snap as a bullet hits the concrete wall of Tía Carmen's house. Pepito, Manuelito, and I instinctively duck our heads, and Mami shouts a word she's smacked me on the back of the head before for saying. Laughter erupts outside along with shouts of "¡Patria o muerte!"

Manuelito, Pepito, and I try to line up the dominoes again, but our hands shake too hard. The tiles keep falling over prematurely. Manuelito gives up and starts gnawing on his fingernails.

A sharp knock interrupts our game, and Tía Carmen opens the door. A man in green fatigues stands in the doorway. His black, greasy beard glistens in the candlelight coming from the kitchen.

"Good evening, compañera. Wonderful evening

for the revolution, no?" he sneers, looking Tía Carmen up and down.

She crosses her arms in front of her. "What do you want?"

The soldier raises his eyebrow. "You hear we defeated the Yanquis?"

"Everyone's heard your nonsense." Tía Carmen clicks her tongue and stares hard at the soldier.

From the kitchen, Mami hisses, "¡Carmencita! ¡Tranquila!"

The soldier pushes past Tía Carmen, the rifle slung over his shoulder smacking against the doorframe. He stands over us sitting at the kitchen table with our dominoes. My palms start to sweat and stick to the plastic tablecloth.

"You boys should be proud. You have witnessed the power of the revolution over the Yanquis. The power of Cuba over the imperialists," he declares, hands on his hips.

Tía Carmen rolls her eyes, and Mami elbows her hard in the ribs.

The soldier turns on his heels and stands an inch from Mami. "You know, compañera, the revolution is always seeking young men for the cause of freedom."

Mami grips the kitchen towel in her hands until I think her knuckles will burst through her skin. I crane my neck to see her face, but the thick stock of the soldier's rifle is in the way. My heartbeat pounds in my ears, making it nearly impossible to hear what he is saying.

"Do you need anything, compañero?" Mami asks, clearing her throat. I know she's trying to distract the soldier from his current line of thought. In the last few weeks, rumors have grown about boys my age and older being shipped off to the Soviet Union to train for the military. Last week, Ladislao Pérez quit coming to school, and Pepito swears he's on a boat headed straight for Moscow. I might think that wasn't true if it weren't for the soldiers' hungry eyes sizing me up every time I walk past the garrison.

The soldier runs his hand through his inky beard. "A glass of water. It's hard work celebrating our victory."

The soldier winks at Mami, and my stomach churns.

Mami fills a glass and hands it to him so quickly water sloshes out onto the tile floor.

The soldier takes a long drink, water droplets sitting in the curls of his coarse beard. He saunters over to our table. "You need a fourth," he says, picking up a tile. The soldier slams his glass onto the table and sets his rifle against the empty chair. The black barrel points at an angle toward Pepito. I grip the table hard, staring at Mami.

She hurries over to us and places both hands on Pepito's shoulders. "They were just about to go to bed," she says, her voice fluttering.

The soldier flips a tile between his fingers and looks at me with black eyes. "And how old are you?"

I swallow hard, almost forgetting my age. "Twelve," I manage.

The soldier places his hand on top of my head and ruffles my hair. His hand is heavy and hot. Mami's grip on Pepito's shoulders tightens.

A sneer grows across the soldier's face. "I imagine we'll be seeing you at the garrison soon. All the sons of Cuba must do their part."

Hot liquid rises in my throat. I think I might throw up.

The shouts increase outside, and the soldier tosses the tile onto the table. He slings his rifle back over his shoulder. Brushing past Tía Carmen and Mami, he exits into the night with a raised fist and a shout of "¡Venceremos!"

I pick up the soldier's discarded tile and flip it over in my hand. Eighteen dots stare up at me like a spray of bullet holes.

The dead man's box.

CHAPTER 2

"If your mami sees that cat, she'll string you up by your toes and dangle you over a pit of crocodiles. You know that, right?"

My friend Serapio punches me in the arm and winks. He shoves another ajonjoli into his mouth, the sesame seeds and sugar leaving a sticky trail at the corner of his lips.

The brown tabby cat purrs and rubs against the leg of my black pants, making me trip on the dirt road as Serapio and I walk home from school. It jumped out as we passed the post office and followed us, hoping Serapio would drop some of his sesame candy.

"Oye, Cumbito," Serapio says. "I've got a winner for AFDF."

I'm not really in the mood to play our usual game of Antes de Fidel, Después de Fidel, where we try to top each other with the most ridiculous ways our lives have changed from before Fidel to after Fidel. I rub my thumb over the domino tile in the pocket of my pants. I've kept the dead man's box tile with me ever since the soldier tossed it onto the table in Tía Carmen's kitchen last week. We returned to our house the next day, Papi emerging from the back bedroom, dark circles under his eyes revealing his long night of sleeplessness and worry. The tile pressed into my leg as my arms cramped from hugging Papi tighter and tighter, fearing he'd disappear if I let go. Since then, Mami and Papi have tried to act like everything is normal, but each time I close my eyes, I feel the soldier's heavy hand on my head and his snarling voice inviting me to the garrison.

"Mira, it's the best," Serapio continues. "So, before Fidel, we had regular chickens."

He pauses and raises his eyebrow at me, expecting me to say something.

"And what do we have after Fidel?" I humor him and ask.

Serapio grins. "After Fidel, we have socialist chickens. They poop in everyone's yard equally."

Serapio's laugh bounces off the stone wall we're walking past, and I groan. I don't offer my submission to Serapio's game because all I can think of is that before Fidel, my family wasn't hiding in fear.

After Fidel, I jump every time I hear the stomp of a soldier's boot on the street.

"Oye, Cumbito. I'm telling you. That cat has mal de ojo. Your mother is going to lose her mind," Serapio mumbles as bits of candy fly from his mouth.

He tries to shoo the cat away, but his hands are covered with sticky sugar syrup from the ajonjoli. He only succeeds in getting brown fur stuck to his fingers.

I shrug. "Doesn't matter if this cat has the evil eye. It could hold an allegiance rally to Mami with all the animals in Cuba and she'd still run screaming for the hills."

"I've never met anyone as scared of animals as your mami."

"Tell me about it. She almost burned the house down that one time Pepito brought three lizards home."

The cat darts behind my legs as a cluster of scowling soldiers shoves six men toward the garrison with their rifles. Yellow shirts hang from the prisoners' slumped shoulders as they shuffle in a line, faces downcast and arms tied behind their backs.

I grab Serapio's arm. "Wait. They're marching more prisoners."

Serapio scans the faces of the men, his fists

clenched and his face white. "You don't think my dad . . . ?"

He swallows hard instead of finishing his sentence.

I shake my head. "No. I don't see him."

Ever since the failed Bay of Pigs invasion a week ago, the government has been rounding up the exiles who fought and anyone else who helped them. A whisper from the Committee for the Defense of the Revolution and you land yourself a yellow shirt and spot in jail.

Serapio's dad was one of the invaders.

We continue down the street, avoiding the prisoners. We pass a tall stone wall, dented and marked with bullet holes. I don't think about what was between the guns and the wall.

The cat abandons its ajonjoli mission and makes a new mission to rub as much fur on my pant leg as it possibly can. I can feel Mami's smack on the back of my head already.

I turn the corner at my street, hoping the cat will continue with Serapio toward his home, but it sticks with me. I pause a block from my house and try to brush off as much of the cat hair from my pants as I can. The cat looks at me with amusement. It heads over to a wall where the Committee for the

Defense of the Revolution has glued up new posters. ¡HASTA LA VICTORIA, SIEMPRE! scream large letters over the image of a bearded man in green fatigues and a beret. The cat stretches upward and drags its claws along the bottom row of posters, tearing one down the middle.

I'm starting to like this cat. HASTA LOS GATOS, SIEMPRE, if you ask me.

I go in the side gate and through the backyard to our kitchen. We never enter through the front of our house because that's where Mami runs her dental practice. The front room of our house is filled with a dentist chair, a desk, and all of Mami's tools. We know not to disturb anything.

And definitely not to let any animals in.

When I enter the kitchen, our maid, Aracelia, is singing at the kitchen sink, her dark curls bouncing along with her hips. Pepito sits at the table behind her, sneaking galletas from a plate on the table. I understand now why he didn't wait for me after school and rushed home before I could catch him. He remembered today was Aracelia's usual day to make cookies.

I brush my hand along the corners of my mouth to show Pepito he has evidence he needs to get rid of. He winks and reaches for another cookie.

Aracelia turns from the sink. "¡Ay, niño! What are you thinking?" she exclaims, waving her hands.

Thinking she's caught Pepito the Cookie Thief, I laugh. Then I feel a warm body brush against my leg.

The cat followed me into the kitchen.

"Por Dios, get that thing out of here right now! Did you mail your brain to the United States?"

Aracelia waves a dish towel at the cat, but it bats its brown paws at the dangling cloth.

I pick up the cat, tossing it outside. It gives me a dirty look, then saunters down the street.

Turning back to the kitchen, I spot Pepito nabbing another cookie. "Would it help to say the cat ripped up a poster of Comandante Che?"

Aracelia sighs. "That's all we need. An antirevolutionary cat in the house."

Pepito chuckles, and cookie crumbs spray from his mouth.

Aracelia puts her hands on her hips and lowers her eyes at Pepito. "If I remember correctly, there were ten galletas on this plate. Niños, you're both worse than el cucuy."

I scuff my feet on the floor. In my opinion, there are worse things to be afraid of now than stolen cookies, stray cats, and the boogeyman. The bullet-marked walls and marching prisoners remind me every time I walk to and from school.

Pepito shoves the plate of cookies away when he sees Mami and Papi enter the kitchen. Papi's linen suit hangs on his thin frame. He takes off his hat, running his hand through his slicked-back hair. Papi opens his mouth to greet us but shakes his head and closes his lips. He shuffles down the hall to their bedroom, shoulders hunched and head bowed.

I start to ask Mami what's wrong, but she claps her hands together. "Bueno, niños. How was school?"

Pepito points a finger and looks at me with devilish eyes. "Cumba brought a cat home."

One of these days, I'm going to design a house and put Pepito's room in a hole in the backyard.

"Pepito probably won't need dinner, Mami. He's been stealing cookies from Aracelia."

Mami shakes her head. "Ay, I should sign you both up for the Committee. You're too good at telling on others."

There's no way I'd ever work for the Committee for the Defense of the Revolution. First, their name is completamente ridículo. Second, they're just a bunch of tattletales that spy on their neighbors and report to the government. Buy meat on the black market? The Committee will report you. Listen to antirevolutionary radio La Voz de las Americas? The Committee will report you.

Manuelito would probably jump at the chance. Last week he told Tía Carmen that Mami traded extra sugar rations for Doña Teresa's teeth cleaning.

The sound of Papi's clarinet flows down the hallway from his bedroom, and for a moment, we are all swept up in Brahms's clarinet trio. The sad notes swirl around the kitchen, and the song increases speed. It sounds like a storm rolling in from the ocean.

Papi played in the orchestra when Presidente Batista was still in power. Now there's no more orchestra. No more music. The song Papi plays usually has a piano and cello as well. Now it's only Papi.

I wander down the hallway, past pictures of Mami and Papi on their wedding day, Pepito as a chubby baby, and me as a skinny baby.

I open the door to Mami and Papi's room and see Papi sitting on the bed. Standing in the doorway, I watch him play. With each breath, his shoulders rise and he sways the clarinet from side to side. At the last note, he lifts the end of the instrument in the air, filling the room with sound. Finishing the song, he lowers the clarinet to his thigh and sits in silence.

"That was good, Papi," I offer.

Startled, he turns and looks at me. I notice tears at the corners of his dark eyes. "Gracias, niño."

He pats the bed, and I move to sit next to him, putting my head on his shoulder. He wraps his arm around me and envelops me in the smell of tobacco and oaky cologne. We watch the tocororo jump from branch to branch on the mango tree outside the bedroom window. Its red, blue, and white feathers match the colors of the Cuban flag. It hops to the ground to pick at a fallen mango.

A scream from the kitchen breaks our silence, and the tocororo flies away.

"¡Ay! ¡Me está mirando!"

The cat must've wandered back into the house. And now Mami is screaming because it's looking at her.

I get up to save Mami from the feline apocalypse, but Papi puts his hand on my shoulder.

"Niño, 'pérate," he says.

I sit back down on the bed. Papi reaches into his pocket and takes out a piece of paper. It's been folded and unfolded so many times it's about to fall apart at the creases.

Papi hands me the paper, and I begin to read.

All sons and daughters of Cuba must do their duty for

the glorious revolution . . . Pioneers against imperialism must train . . . Military service is required of Cuba's children . . .

My heart pounds in my throat, and black spots float in my eyes, keeping me from reading further.

Papi lowers his head and mutters, "They say they're sending children to the Soviet Union for military training."

The hot breeze from the open window sticks to my skin, and my chest heaves, trying to catch a breath.

Swallowing hard, I look at my dad. "Papi, no quiero ir. ¡No quiero ir!"

Papi grabs my hand and squeezes it. "Don't worry. You aren't going. I will not sacrifice my son to Fidel."

He clears his throat and stares out the window. "You're going to the United States."

CHAPTER 3

When Fidel came down from the mountains, the birds flew away. And along with them went President Batista.

Now, instead of birds, we have whispers. Whispers about the government. Whispers about neighbors. They swirl through the air and tickle up your spine. Abuelo whispers that Fidel Castro and Che Guevara aren't heroes for kicking out Cuba's last corrupt president two years ago. Mami whispers that the tanks Fidel rolled down the streets of Havana in victory have now turned against the Cuban people. Neighbors whisper that anyone who flees the island under Fidel's heavy fist is a gusano. A worm and a cobarde.

If I leave, will that make me a coward, too?

My teacher, Padre Tomás, clears his throat and snaps me from my thoughts. "As you can see, estudiantes, when the government owns all the farmland, it can make sure all resources are shared equally."

Padre Tomás rolls his eyes as he says this. His thick black glasses magnify his eyeballs. It's like watching a frog spot a fly on the ceiling. The Cuban government mandates what Padre Tomás can teach, even in a Catholic school, so we've suffered through lectures about agrarian reform and the dangers of foreign influence.

Serapio taps my shoulder and points to the platform at the front of the classroom where Padre Tomás's desk is perched.

"Oye, Cumbito. Today's the day. I can feel it," he says, his brown eyes sparkling with mischief.

Each day before school, Serapio slides Padre Tomás's desk closer to the edge of the platform. Today the front legs of the desk hang an inch over the platform. One good push on a drawer and the desk will topple off the platform and crash to the floor.

My friend Geraldo sits in front of me, and I nudge him in the back. "Get ready, Geraldito. It's gonna happen today."

Geraldo shrugs and reaches into his desk. When Padre Tomás turns toward the chalkboard, Geraldo pulls out a bocadito and takes a bite, bread crumbs and bits of ham falling onto his black uniform pants.

"Oye, Amarito," I whisper to my friend next to me. "Wait for it."

Amaro ignores me. He tries to balance a pencil on his nose but pokes himself in the eye with the tip.

Padre Tomás faces us again, his blond hair slowly fading from the top of his forehead, retreating from the fifteen mischievous sixth-grade boys who torture him daily. Well, maybe not all fifteen of us. Mostly just Serapio.

"Bueno, estudiantes. Do you have any questions over our review of the government's new agricultural measures?" Padre Tomás asks.

Serapio's hand shoots up in the air. The smirk on his face grows.

Ay Dios mío, here we go.

Serapio stands next to his desk and clears his throat. "Padre Bobo, is it true the government is sending students to the countryside to teach? ¿Qué demonios es eso?"

Geraldo chuckles and nearly chokes on his bocadito. Amaro and I have to cover our mouths to keep from laughing.

We found out the first week of school that our Canadian teacher learned Spanish through the Catholic Church. This means he never learned any of those interesting words that usually earn us cocotazos on the back of the head from our mothers. Serapio takes advantage of this and seasons his questions and answers with choice words.

"That's true, Serapio. The government is sending Los Jóvenes Rebeldes to smaller towns in the country."

I look at Amaro. He already knows the answer to Serapio's question. His older brother, Eugenio, was sent by the Young Rebels to a small town near Camagüey to teach patriotismo. But Amaro ignores the conversation and tries to touch his tongue to his nose.

Padre Tomás shuffles over to his desk and opens the top drawer. Serapio and I lean in, our hands clenching our desks in anticipation. Padre Tomás takes out some blank cards from his desk. "These cards are for the Committee for the Defense of the Revolution," he says, holding them up for the class to see.

Padre Tomás's hand rests on the drawer. Serapio and I clench our desks tighter, waiting for him to close it. Instead, he takes off his glasses and rubs his eyes. "Actually, jóvenes," Padre Tomás says, his voice cracking, "I'm supposed to tell you to write down anything you see that would be considered against the Cuban government's new goals. But I just don't think—"

Padre Tomás shuts the drawer of his desk. It's just enough force to send the desk toppling over the platform. It crashes to the floor of our classroom with a thunderous bang. Fifteen boys jump back.

Shouts and laughter fill the classroom. Serapio stands next to his desk again and takes a bow.

I clap for my crazy friend but look at the front of the classroom, where Padre Tomás is standing above his damaged desk. The cards in his hand flutter to the floor, and he once again removes his glasses to rub his eyes.

The school bell rings, declaring the end of the day and saving Padre Tomás from further humiliation. And, more important, saving Serapio from punishment. We tumble out of the classroom, a hurricane of cackles and slaps on the back.

I head to the school courtyard to meet up with Pepito before we walk home.

"Your papi get tired of hiding?" a voice snarls behind me.

I turn and see Manuelito leaning against a column, his eyes narrowed and a scowl growing across his face.

"He probably looks good in yellow shirts, doesn't he?"

I march over to him, stopping an inch from his face. Manuelito may be only a year younger than I am, but I'm about half a foot taller.

"At least my dad still lives on the island," I hiss, looking down on him.

Manuelito opens his mouth to say something, but no sound comes out. "But . . . but," he finally stammers.

I jab my finger into his chest. "Quit talking tontería about my dad. It's not *his* fault your dad left for the United States. And it's not *my* fault your dad didn't return."

Manuelito's cheeks turn red, tears welling up in his eyes. I take a step back. I know I've said too much, but Manuelito picked the wrong day to mess with me.

Shoving my hands into my pockets, I feel the ever-present bumps of the caja de muertos domino. I turn away from Manuelito and walk across the courtyard, spotting Pepito at the entrance gate.

"¿Cómo anda, Cumbito?" Pepito asks.

I pat him on the back. "Well, Serapito finally got Padre Tomás's desk to nose-dive off the platform. He'd been moving it for two weeks."

Pepito laughs. "Ay, poor Padre Tomás. What a going-away present."

I look at Pepito. "Going away? What do you mean?"

"Padre Francisco told us that Fidel is kicking out all the yuma priests. Any priest from another country has to leave," Pepito explains.

On the scale of sins, I wonder how high torturing a priest ranks. Is it worse than letting a friend forget his troubles by amusing himself? Amaro, Geraldo, and I have indulged Serapio's mischief ever since his father disappeared before the Bay of Pigs invasion. Serapio said he thought his dad went to Florida, but his abuela hadn't heard anything.

"Oye, Cumbito," Pepito says, kicking a pebble down the street. "I thought of a good one for AFDF."

I roll my eyes. Pepito always wants to play with us.

"Okay, so before Fidel, I could buy American magazines with cowboys and movie stars," Pepito says, his voice lowered to a whisper so nosy neighbors can't hear.

"I know," I tell him. "What do you think is plastered all over the walls on your side of our room?"

Pepito smiles. "Right. But after Fidel, all we have are Russian magazines in Spanish that tell you everything you never wanted to know about sugarcane farms. This is easily the worst."

I can't help but chuckle. Of all the injustices Fidel and his government have imposed on us, of course Pepito thinks his lack of access to American cowboys is the cruelest of all.

Pepito and I head toward home. We pass Doña Teresa's house, and out jumps a familiar brown tabby cat.

"¡Demonio!" Pepito shouts, crouching down and petting the cat.

"You named the cat 'Demon'?" I ask.

Pepito raises an eyebrow and smiles as the cat purrs against his leg. "Don't you think Mami would agree?"

I put my hands on my hips. "With the name? Yes. With the cat? No way. We'd better lose it before we get home."

"It's not my fault he keeps coming around," Pepito says as we continue our walk home. Despite my attempts to shoo him away, Demonio weaves between our legs.

We pass Parque Vidal in the center of town. Pepito reaches into his pocket and pulls out a piece of crema de leche. He drops it to the ground, and Demonio snaps it up, licking his lips.

I sigh. "Any chance this cat keeps coming around because you keep feeding him candy?"

Pepito smirks and crosses his chest with his finger. "I'm a saint, mal rayo me parta."

I laugh and shake my head. Pepito is always swearing upon penalty of lightning strike. I think of Padre Tomás. If anyone deserves to be struck by lightning, it's probably me.

Maybe I could stand right next to Fidel.

"Mira, Pepito. This cat can't follow us home again. Mami's got too much on her mind lately."

Pepito looks down. "Because you're leaving?"

I start to correct Pepito, to tell him he shouldn't talk about that because the whispers might snatch it up. And talking about it makes something real that so far has only existed in the foggy gray swirl of my dreams.

But a figure crossing the road in front of us catches my eye. Led by soldiers on either side, the man straightens his shoulders and keeps step with his escorts. It isn't until he adjusts his hat that I see who the man is.

Papi.

I stumble, and my hand hits a bullet-marked wall to regain my balance. We thought that Papi was safe after the Bay of Pigs. The government seemed not to care that he went back to being a regular lawyer, which he did after his military service for Batista.

But did they change their minds? What were they doing with Papi?

I grab Pepito's arm and pull him down the street behind Papi and the soldiers. We stay far enough away that I can still see Papi's fists clench as the soldiers at his sides grip the straps of the rifles slung over their shoulders.

It's only when they turn the corner near the post office that I realize where they're headed.

After Fidel took power, Mami and Papi told me and Pepito to never go near the prison in Santa Clara. The small, one-story building with a walled courtyard seemed innocent enough, but Fidel was filling it with anyone he thought opposed the revolution.

Had the whispers finally reached Papi? Had they slithered around his wrists like shackles?

"Cumba, where are we going?" Pepito whines, dragging his feet. I don't want to tell him who we're following because I don't want him to be as scared as I am.

The soldiers push Papi into the prison courtyard and slam a heavy metal gate behind them, the sharp sound echoing down the street.

Pepito yanks his hand from mine, his eyes darting across the walls of the prison. "We're not supposed to be here. Mami and Papi said. What are you doing?"

I swallow hard and try to make my voice as calm as possible. "I need to see something. Don't worry."

I pull Pepito over to a tall jaguey tree looming over the wall surrounding the prison courtyard, and he crouches between the large, drooping roots, a scowl on his face. I scramble up the tree and perch myself in its branches, just above the wall but hidden from the soldiers in the courtyard.

Papi stands with one soldier. A few others smoke cigars and laugh as they load their rifles.

Two soldiers emerge from inside the prison, dragging a man about Abuelo's age between them. His crumpled clothes are marked with dirt. I search his face, the wrinkles that spread from his dark eyes, his lips pulled in a tight line, to see if I recognize him. But I don't. He's just another person who made Fidel angry.

My fingers dig into the bark of the jaguey tree as the soldiers shove the old man to a bare wall of the prison.

The soldier next to Papi sneers and says, "Compañero Fernandez, we are so grateful to have a lawyer of your fine standing in our town."

The soldier sounds anything but thankful, and the smirk plastered on his face reveals his sarcasm.

"Your presence here today for these proceedings will confirm that the revolution is fair and just." The soldier's lip curls into a snarl under the curly black hair of his beard.

I watch as Papi holds his hat in his hand, his knuckles about to tear the cream fabric in two. He opens his mouth to speak, but the old man gives Papi the slightest nod. Papi's shoulders sag, and he mumbles something to the soldier that I can't make out.

My eyes lock on Papi as the soldiers finish loading their rifles. I notice tears glistening in the corners of his eyes as the sun looms lower on the horizon.

I want to run to Papi and pull him away from the courtyard. I want to take the old man with us and hide him in our house.

A line of rifles forms in front of the old man, and my stomach rolls. Pepito kicks the dirt below me, and I hear him start to scramble up the tree.

"Don't come up here," I tell him, unable to hide the edge in my voice. "Stay down there. Just stay down there."

That's when the singing starts.

The old man stands against the wall, his shoulders square and his chest puffed out as he sings "La Bayamesa," the Cuban national anthem. The notes float over the soldiers, across the courtyard, and rustle the leaves of the jaguey tree.

Do not fear a glorious death.

The soldier next to Papi shouts, and the firing squad readies their rifles.

For to die for the homeland is to live.

Another shout and the soldiers aim their rifles. Pepito's hand grabs my ankle as he climbs up the tree.

To live in chains is to live

Mired in shame and disgrace.

One final shout and a series of cracks puncture the air. The singing stops. Pepito's eyes grow wide, and his mouth drops open as he peeks over the wall.

"No!" I yell, pushing him away from the sight. We lose our grips and tumble from the tree, landing in a tangle of limbs with a hard thud in the dirt.

The leaves of the jaguey tree hang still, no longer rustled by the old man's song. The prison gate creaks, and heavy footsteps scuff in the dirt away from us.

Pepito trembles in my arms as his tears soak my shirt.

"I want to go home," he whimpers.

I keep my arm tight around his shoulders, making sure to put myself between Pepito and the prison. Legs shaking, we make our way back down the street, toward our house.

As the soldiers behind us in the prison begin shouting at one another, I can't help but wonder who will take care of Pepito after I fly away.